"Which way did the man on the big gray go?"

The man thought a moment, then said, "North."

"Thanks."

"And so did the other man."

"The other man?" Clint turned Eclipse back to the man. "What other man?"

"The one who left soon after your friend."

"What'd he look like?"

"Thirties, kinda thick, not as tall as you."

"And he rode in the same direction?"

"Yup."

"Did he say anything?"

"Nope. Neither of them did. They just . . . left."

"Anything else you can tell me?"

The man shrugged. "Your friend carried a big buffalo gun," he said. "Other fella a Winchester and a sidearm. That's about it."

"Okay," Clint said. "Thanks."

"Good luck to you."

Clint turned Eclipse, and rode north.

DON'T MISS THESE
ALL-ACTION WESTERN SERIES
FROM THE BERKLEY PUBLISHING GROUP

THE GUNSMITH by J. R. Roberts

Clint Adams was a legend among lawmen, outlaws, and ladies. They called him . . . the Gunsmith.

LONGARM by Tabor Evans

The popular long-running series about Deputy U.S. Marshal Custis Long—his life, his loves, his fight for justice.

SLOCUM by Jake Logan

Today's longest-running action Western. John Slocum rides a deadly trail of hot blood and cold steel.

BUSHWHACKERS by B. J. Lanagan

An action-packed series by the creators of Longarm! The rousing adventures of the most brutal gang of cutthroats ever assembled—Quantrill's Raiders.

DIAMONDBACK by Guy Brewer

Dex Yancey is Diamondback, a Southern gentleman turned con man when his brother cheats him out of the family fortune. Ladies love him. Gamblers hate him. But nobody pulls one over on Dex . . .

WILDGUN by Jack Hanson

The blazing adventures of mountain man Will Barlow—from the creators of Longarm!

TEXAS TRACKER by Tom Calhoun

J.T. Law: the most relentless—and dangerous—manhunter in all Texas. Where sheriffs and posses fail, he's the best man to bring in the most vicious outlaws—for a price.

THE GUNSMITH

356

HUNT FOR THE WHITE WOLF

J. R. ROBERTS

JOVE BOOKS, NEW YORK

THE BERKLEY PUBLISHING GROUP
Published by the Penguin Group
Penguin Group (USA) Inc.
375 Hudson Street, New York, New York 10014, USA

Penguin Group (Canada), 90 Eglinton Avenue East, Suite 700, Toronto, Ontario M4P 2Y3, Canada
(a division of Pearson Penguin Canada Inc.)
Penguin Books Ltd., 80 Strand, London WC2R 0RL, England
Penguin Group Ireland, 25 St. Stephen's Green, Dublin 2, Ireland (a division of Penguin Books Ltd.)
Penguin Group (Australia), 250 Camberwell Road, Camberwell, Victoria 3124, Australia
(a division of Pearson Australia Group Pty. Ltd.)
Penguin Books India Pvt. Ltd., 11 Community Centre, Panchsheel Park, New Delhi—110 017, India
Penguin Group (NZ), 67 Apollo Drive, Rosedale, Auckland 0632, New Zealand
(a division of Pearson New Zealand Ltd.)
Penguin Books (South Africa) (Pty.) Ltd., 24 Sturdee Avenue, Rosebank, Johannesburg 2196,
South Africa

Penguin Books Ltd., Registered Offices: 80 Strand, London WC2R 0RL, England

This is a work of fiction. Names, characters, places, and incidents either are the product of the author's imagination or are used fictitiously, and any resemblance to actual persons, living or dead, business establishments, events, or locales is entirely coincidental.

HUNT FOR THE WHITE WOLF

A Jove Book / published by arrangement with the author

PRINTING HISTORY
Jove edition / August 2011

Copyright © 2011 by Robert J. Randisi.
Cover illustration by Sergio Giovine.

All rights reserved.
No part of this book may be reproduced, scanned, or distributed in any printed or electronic form without permission. Please do not participate in or encourage piracy of copyrighted materials in violation of the author's rights. Purchase only authorized editions.
For information, address: The Berkley Publishing Group,
a division of Penguin Group (USA) Inc.,
375 Hudson Street, New York, New York 10014.

ISBN: 978-0-515-14974-6

JOVE®
Jove Books are published by The Berkley Publishing Group,
a division of Penguin Group (USA) Inc.,
375 Hudson Street, New York, New York 10014.
JOVE® is a registered trademark of Penguin Group (USA) Inc.
The "J" design is a trademark of Penguin Group (USA) Inc.

PRINTED IN THE UNITED STATES OF AMERICA

10 9 8 7 6 5 4 3 2 1

If you purchased this book without a cover, you should be aware that this book is stolen property. It was reported as "unsold and destroyed" to the publisher, and neither the author nor the publisher has received any payment for this "stripped book."

ONE

Jesse Trapp entered the White Wolf Saloon and laid his Big Fifty on the bar.

"Beer," he said.

The bartender looked at the rifle, then the man. Trapp was big, slope-shouldered, raw-boned, covered with buffalo skins and hair. He could have been anywhere from sixty to eighty.

"You got money?" the bartender, all of twenty-five, asked.

"I got money, junior," Trapp said.

The bartender sniffed, wondering if the smell was the man or the skins. Probably a combination of both.

"Let's see it."

Trapp stared at the young bartender.

"You got beer?" he asked.

"I got beer."

"So let's see it," Trapp said with a shrug.

The bartender stared at the older man, but in the end

looked away, drew a beer, and brought it over. Trapp put his money on the bar, picked up the beer, and drank it down. He wiped his mouth with the back of his hand.

"Whaddaya use a gun that big for?" the bartender asked.

"Well, I tell ya, son," Trapp said, "used ta be I kilt buffler with it, then I kilt some Injuns with it. Nowadays I kill wolves."

"Wolves."

"Yessir," Trapp said. "Like the one this place is named fer."

"You've killed white wolves?" the young man said with wide eyes.

"I have, indeed," Trapp said. "Several, in fact."

"And what are ya doin' now?"

"I'm on my way to kill another wolf," Trapp said.

"A white one?"

"Naw, just a regular old gray wolf been killin' some stock and some folks north of here. Seems the folks there can't kill it themselves, so they sent fer me. I was passin' thru yer town, saw the name of this place, and decided to have me a beer, here."

"You want another one?"

"Sure. Lemme show ya my money, though." He reached into his skins.

"Naw, never mind," the kid said. "This one's on the house."

"Well, thank ya kindly."

The young man put another beer in front of Trapp and said, "Couldja tell me a story about killin' a wolf?"

"I got plenty of stories."

"About a white wolf?"

"You wanna story 'bout killin' a white wolf?"

"Yessir."

"Seems one of them boiled eggs in that bowl there might make me more likely ta tell a story like that," Trapp said.

The bartender grabbed an egg from the bowl, then grabbed a second one. He put them down in front of Trapp, who picked one up and started to peel it.

"Hey, Ben!" the bartender called across the room to another man his age. "This fella's gonna tell a story about killin' a white wolf."

"Oh, yeah?" Ben said. He picked up his beer and carried it over. "He sure looks like he could kill a white wolf. You mind if I listen, too, mister?"

"Naw, I don't mind at all, sonny," Trapp said. He bit into his egg, closed one eye, and thought a moment before speaking.

"Lemme see, seems the first one was nigh onto forty years ago . . ."

Sitting in a corner a man nursed a beer and listened while Jesse Trapp told stories about not only himself, but his older brother, John Henry. It was when he heard that name that the man's ears really perked up. He leaned back in his seat, eased his gun in and out of his holster to make sure it was loose.

It had been years since the man had heard the name John Henry Trapp. He'd hunted the man for years, finally came to the conclusion that it was only by not hunting him that he'd find him. After twelve years, he'd almost given up hope, but stopping in this saloon in a one-horse Wyoming town had done the trick.

Jesse Trapp had walked right into his arms. And could maybe lead him straight to John Henry.

TWO

Three men entered the White Wolf Saloon and looked around.

"This place is dead," one of them said.

"As long as it's got beer," the second said.

"And whiskey," the third said.

They walked to the bar, took up a position far from Trapp—but not far enough to avoid the smell.

"Oh my God," Dean Wister said. "What is that smell?"

"Whoa!" Sam Bolden exclaimed, fanning the air. "Somethin' die in here?"

"Can we get a drink down here?" Charlie Mead yelled to the bartender.

"Right there," the bartender said, then to Trapp, "Hey, don't let me miss anythin'."

He moved down the bar. "What'll ya have?"

"Two whiskeys and three beers," Mead said. He knew his partners liked a whiskey with a beer chaser—or maybe the other way around—but he preferred just beer.

"Comin' up."

The bartender poured out the two whiskeys, then carried the three beers over.

"Is that smell comin' from that character at the other end of the bar?" Wister asked.

"Ain't so bad, once ya get used to it," the barman said.

"I don't wanna get used to it," Bolden said. "I want it to go away."

"'scuse me," the bartender said. "I was listenin' to a story."

"A story?" Bolden asked as the bartender moved away. "That smelly hombre's tellin' stories?"

"Probably tradin' stories for eggs and beer," Mead said. "I seen fellas do it before."

"Yeah, me, too," Bolden said, "but not with that smell."

"We gotta get him outta here," Wister said, "or I'm gonna puke."

"Leave him be," Mead said. "Drink your drink and we'll get outta here."

"I ain't leavin'," Wister said. "That jasper is. And if he don't leave, I'm gonna give him a bath."

He drank his whiskey, picked up his beer, and walked down to where Jesse Trapp was standing, still telling stories and peeling eggs. There was a small pile of eggshells on the bar.

"'Scuse me," he said, tapping Trapp on his shoulder.

The older man turned and said, "I'm in the middle of somethin', son. Can it wait?"

When Trapp turned back to his audience Wister poked

him again and said, "No, it can't wait. I'll probably die from the smell by then."

"Then why don't ya hold yer breath?" Trapp asked. "It'll only be eight or ten more minutes."

Wister turned and looked at his two partners, then removed Trapp's hat and poured the contents of his beer mug over the man's head.

"There," he said, "maybe that'll take care of the smell for eight or ten minutes."

Trapp turned around and stared at Wister for a moment. The man was thirty years or so younger, taller, but slighter. When Trapp hit him he went flying across the room, landing on his butt in the sawdust of the floor.

"Whoa!" Charlie Mead said, impressed.

While Wister was the fighter of the three, Sam Bolden was the gunman. He pushed away from the bar and faced Trapp.

"Hey!" he said.

"Don't," Trapp said.

"Don't, Sam," Mead said from behind Bolden.

Trapp put his right hand on the bar.

"Wait!" Wister said.

They all looked at him.

"He's mine." Wister got to his feet, but didn't bother to brush himself off. He removed his jacket and tossed it on a table. He was more slender than Trapp but well muscled.

"Hey—" the bartender started.

"Quiet!" Bolden said. "Go ahead, Dean."

Trapp eyed Bolden, wondering if he would really stay out of it.

Dean Wister advanced on Trapp, who stood his ground.

"Lucky punch, old man," Wister said with a tight grin. "Let's see what you think of this."

Wister launched a right hook at Trapp's head. The old mountain man caught it in his left, and the two stood there for a moment, frozen, until Trapp started to squeeze. Wister felt the incredible strength of the older man crushing his hand.

"Ouch," Wister said. "Kill 'im, Sam."

Sam Bolden went for his gun, but Trapp put his right hand on the bar, found the trigger of his Big Fifty, and pulled it. A .50-caliber piece of lead punched right through Bolden, took out most of his back, and barely missed Mead, although it did splatter him with his friend's blood.

"Jesus!"

"How about you?" Trapp asked him. He then looked at Wister again. "Your turn?"

"Take it easy, mister!" Wister said, holding one hand out in front of him. Trapp kept his eye on the other hand, just in case.

The bartender laid a shotgun barrel on the bar. "Okay, boys. On your way."

Mead and Wister looked at the bartender, then at Trapp, and then at the body of their friend.

"Pick him up and take him with you," the bartender said.

Wister came over next to Mead. Together they picked up Bolden's body, holding it between them.

"Hurry up," the bartender said, "he's still gettin' blood on the floor."

The two men backed toward the door awkwardly, then turned and went out, dragging the body between them.

"Thanks, friend," Trapp said to the bartender.

"I wasn't sure whether or not they knew," the barman said, "that you had to load that Big Fifty again before you could use it."

"Ha!" Trapp laughed. But he did take the time to eject the spent shell and insert a new one before he continued his stories.

The man in the corner was impressed with the way Jesse Trapp dispatched the three men, only having to kill one of them.

Now he knew he wouldn't be able to take the man on his own. He'd been toying with the idea of taking him right there and then in the saloon. He was grateful to the three men for changing his mind.

He got up, walked to the bar, and asked the bartender for another beer. He stood a few feet down from Trapp, who was still telling stories. The bartender gave him a beer while still listening. He took a moment to size Trapp up. Standing behind him, he could have taken the chance and tried to shoot him in the back, but there were too many witnesses for that.

In the end he turned, walked back to his table, sat down, and proceeded to nurse his new beer.

THREE

Clint rode into Little Town, Wyoming, with an amused look on his face. He counted one saloon, one general store, a sheriff's office, one hotel, and one small restaurant. He didn't know if the town was living up to its name, or if it had gotten its name from its size. And it didn't really matter. He was there to meet someone, not to learn about the town.

He bypassed the sheriff's office after briefly considering a stop inside. Instead he rode directly to the saloon, dismounted, and dropped Eclipse's reins to the ground. If anyone tried to walk off—or worse even, ride off—with Eclipse, he'd be sorry. The horse would make sure of that.

He entered the saloon, walked around a bloody spot on the floor, and approached the bar. He looked around, but there were no white wolf pelts on the wall.

"Whaddaya drinkin'?" the bartender asked.

Clint looked at the young man and said, "A nice, cold beer."

"Comin' up."

Clint turned and looked down at the bloodstain on the floor behind him.

"This place must be livelier than it looks," he said as the bartender brought him the beer.

The bartender craned his neck to look at the bloody floor.

"Oh, that," the man said. "That happened a few days ago. A big fella came in here carrying a Sharps Big Fifty—he said he was a wolf hunter."

"Dressed in old buffalo skins?" Clint asked. "Maybe they smelled, maybe he did, but there was definitely a smell?"

"Oh yeah," the bartender said, "and he told—"

"He told stories for beer"—he saw the bowl of eggs on the bar—"and eggs?"

"Yeah," the bartender said. "How did you know? He a friend of yours?"

"Kind of. What happened?"

"Well, these three jaspers came in while he was tellin' us stories, and one them poured a beer on his head."

"He didn't shoot him for that."

"No, in fact, he didn't shoot him at all," the bartender said. "One of the others drew on him, and he beat him—with the Sharps. It was amazing."

"What happened after that?" Clint asked. "Sharps can only fire one bullet at a time, and Trapp doesn't carry a handgun."

"I backed him with my shotgun," the barman said. "Put it up here on the bar, told those jaspers to leave and take their dead friend with them. You know what kind of mess a Big Fifty makes on a man?"

"Why would you do something as dangerous as that?" Clint asked.

The bartender grinned. "He was right in the middle of a story and I wanted to hear the end of it."

The bartender told him that the sheriff had come in after the shooting and taken Trapp to the jail.

"He put him in jail?" Clint asked.

"Nah," the bartender said, "just took him over there for a talk."

So Clint finished his beer, left the saloon, and went over to the sheriff's office after all.

FOUR

"Took me a whole day with the doors and windows open to get rid of the smell," Sheriff Green complained. "The buffalo have been gone a long time. You know how old those skins musta been?"

"Almost as old as him," Clint said.

"Yeah, what about that?" Green asked. "What is he? Sixty? Seventy? Eighty?"

"I don't know," Clint said. "Somewhere in there."

The sheriff shook his head.

"So you didn't put him in a cell because he smelled?" Clint asked.

"Yeah," the lawman said, "but also everybody in the bar said it was a fair fight—if you can call three against one fair."

"I know," Clint said. "He had them outnumbered."

"You think he coulda killed the three of them?" the sheriff asked.

"Easily."

The sheriff raised his eyebrows, impressed. He was in his forties, had been wearing a badge for a while. As soon as Clint had introduced himself the man had recognized his name.

"So, you gonna be stayin' in our little town?" he asked.

"No," Clint said. "I was supposed to meet Jesse Trapp here, but apparently he didn't wait."

"Well," Green said, "I did tell him to get out of town, but I gave him 'til the next mornin'."

"He stayed?"

"At the hotel, I think," Green said, "after a visit to the whorehouse."

"You have a whorehouse?"

"Well, sure," Green said, "a little one."

"What is it with the name?" Clint asked. "Little Town?"

"Not my idea," the sheriff said. "Take any complaints to the town council."

"Can you direct me to the whorehouse?"

The lawman grinned and said, "I'll try."

"The smell wasn't so bad once I got him out of those skins," the whore said. "Also, for a man his age he sure had a lot of stamina. Just about wore me out."

She was in her forties, obviously chosen by Trapp because she was the oldest whore in the house. She had some extra weight on her, but it didn't look bad. She had big breasts that he could see through her filmy top, dark chocolate nipples, long black hair that had a few streaks of gray in it. Her face was lined and puffy, but you could still see the pretty girl she had been. Maybe her face was that way because he'd had to wake her up to talk.

Her name was Angie.

"Of course," she said, "if I could've got him to take a bath . . . but that was askin' too much."

"Did he say where he was going when he left town?" Clint asked.

"We didn't talk much, mister," she said. "Every chance he got he was fuckin' my pussy 'til I screamed. By the time he left, I was sore and exhausted."

"So he went to the hotel from here?"

"I guess. Can I go back to sleep? I'm still pretty tired."

"I guess he made a good choice when he picked you," Clint said.

"Well, it turned out that way, but he worked his way up to me," she said. "He started with the youngest, and none of those girls wanted to go with him. The smell, ya know?"

"Yeah, I know."

"I gotta say," she went on, with a tired smile, "they missed the ride of their life. He wasn't like the usual john who comes in here, ruts for five minutes, and then goes to sleep."

"I'm happy for you." He turned to leave.

"Hey?" she said.

He turned back. She'd pulled the top of her gown down so that her big breasts bobbed free, very round and pale. She flicked her nipples with her thumbs and they started to swell.

"Gimme another hour or two of sleep and then come back."

"I may be busy."

"Hell," she said, tossing back the sheet so he could see her equally pale, smooth thighs and the heavy black pubic thatch between her legs. At that point, he could even smell her. "Hop in here right now then, and we'll get it done."

"Thanks for the offer," he said, "but I never pay for a woman."

"Honey," she said, "I don't remember askin' you for any money."

FIVE

Clint put Eclipse up at the livery, then went to the hotel and checked in. While registering, he found Jesse Trapp's name in the book. Well, actually, he found Trapp's mark. Neither Jesse nor his older brother, John Henry, had ever learned to write, but they had a distinctive enough mark that he was able to tell it was theirs. Most people just made an *X* when they couldn't write, but the Trapps each had their own squiggly kind of mark. Clint could even tell Jesse's from John Henry's.

"You remember this fellow?" Clint asked the clerk.

"Oh, yessir," the young man said. "I remember the smell. We had to clean the room several times and air it out for days."

"He stayed only one day?"

"Thankfully, yes," the man said.

"Did he say where he was heading from here?" Clint asked.

"No, sir, but I didn't really ask."

"All right, thanks."

Clint took his saddlebags and rifle to his room, which was small and clean.

Word had filtered to him through word of mouth that Jesse Trapp was looking for him. The Trapps did not use mode forms of communication like the telegraph. Rather, they used the wind—just send the word out there and it would get where it was going.

Well, Clint had gotten the word that Trapp would be passing through a small town called Little Town, Wyoming, but there was no date. Remarkably, given the dubious way word had been sent to him, he had managed to miss Trapp by just a matter of days.

Jesse's older brother, John Henry, who had spent many years in jail for killing the man who killed his wife, had gone to the mountains when he was released and was still there.

Jesse had become a hunter of animals, mostly wolves and mountain lions, which were terrorizing ranchers. He was good at what he did, and continued to use the old Sharps that he'd hunted buffalo with many years before.

Clint had a general direction. Jesse was riding northwest, maybe headed for Montana. There were lots of wolves in Montana. That was where a man like Jesse Trapp could make a lot of money for himself.

Satisfied with his room, he left and headed over to the saloon again. Maybe he could get some more information from the bartender.

"Well," the bartender said, after serving Clint a beer, "he talked about hunting wolves—told us stories about white wolves. Ya know, I think maybe he said he was on his way to hunt a white wolf."

"You know," Clint said, "white wolves are actually gray wolves. The grays can be a gray, black, or white."

"Is that a fact?"

"I actually learned that from John Henry Trapp, Jesse's brother."

"Well," the bartender said, "he sure was full of stories, but he never mentioned that about the white wolves. I reckon if a wolf is white, then it's a white wolf."

"I guess that makes sense," Clint agreed. "Well, if he's headed for Montana there are plenty of wolves up there. There's plenty of game for the wolves to hunt—moose, elk, deer—and when they're hunting and hungry, wolves are tireless and mean."

"Well," the bartender said, "he tol' me a story about how he wrestled a bear once. Guess he wouldn't have too much trouble with wolves."

"Yep," Clint said, "he wrestled a bear, all right." In his dreams, Clint added to himself.

Clint had supper at Little Town's only restaurant, a small place down the street from the saloon. He'd decided that come morning, he'd just head for Montana. Maybe he'd even pick up Jesse's trail. He'd check at the livery to see if he could pick up what kind of trail Jesse's horse was leaving.

The bartender had told him a story about the town's name. Originally it had been called Littleton, but because it never grew people started referring to it as the "Little Town." The town fathers, in what they thought was a flash of brilliance, decided to rename the place Little Town.

It didn't seem such a stroke of genius to Clint, but he didn't really care. He'd be leaving the town behind him shortly.

He finished his steak, which was a bit tough but edible. The potatoes were good, the carrots undercooked, and the coffee weak. He meant to head back to the saloon for one beer before he returned to his room. But when he got there a poker game was going on at one table. The sheriff stood at the bar, so Clint went up, took up a position next to the lawman, and ordered a beer.

"Buy you one?" he asked.

"Sure, why not?" Green said. "Thanks."

When they both had a beer Clint gestured toward the game.

"They local?" he asked the lawman.

"Yeah, they all are," the man said, "but they're always lookin' for another player. It's low stakes, though."

"That's okay," Clint said. "It's just for something to do."

"Want me to introduce ya?"

"That's okay, I can do it myself."

Clint started for the table, then stopped and looked at the sheriff.

"You pass the word I was in town?"

"Not me," Green said, "but remember, it's a small town."

"Okay, thanks."

He went over to the table, introduced himself as Clint, and sat in.

SIX

Clint ended up staying at the saloon a lot longer than he'd intended. The small-stakes poker game had turned into something interesting. Two of the locals—the man who owned the hotel and the fellow who ran the general store—turned out to be pretty good players. Still, he'd made a small profit and would use it to buy himself a big breakfast in the morning before he got started.

He put the key in the lock of his door, turned it, and froze. Somebody was inside. He wondered why he didn't just put batwing doors on his hotel rooms. People were always coming in and out, and if it wasn't some woman who had taken a liking to him, it was a man who wanted to kill him.

He kept his right hand on his gun, turned the door-knob with his left, and pushed the door open so quickly it slammed against the wall.

The woman on the bed jerked her head, startled, and stared at him with wide eyes.

"Jesus!" she said. "You just about scared me to death."

"Sorry," he said. He stepped inside and looked around. Satisfied that she was the only person in the room, he took his hand off his gun. "What are you doing in my room?"

"Whaddaya think?" she asked. "I'm naked under this sheet."

"I'm sorry, Angie," he said, "I told you earlier I don't pay—"

"And I tol' you I wasn't askin' ya for money," she said. "I'm just wantin' ta fuck. You look fit, and you smell nice."

"Well, thanks, but—"

She removed the sheet to show him her nudity. Those big, pale breasts with the dark brown nipples; plenty of pale, smooth flesh; and that musky smell that rose up from between her thighs.

"Whaddaya say?" she asked.

He removed his gun belt and said, "I say, why not? I mean, you walked all the way over here, right?"

She nodded and said, "And from all the way across town, too."

Being in bed with Angie was almost like a wrestling match. She was lusty, strong, eager, and totally without shame in what she wanted to do and what she wanted done to her.

Clint lost himself in her flesh for hours. He sucked and bit her breasts and nipples, kissed her neck and her mouth and shoulders. He tasted her and experienced her with every sense he had.

At one point he was down between her spread legs, kissing the tender flesh on the inside of her thighs, then moved to the even more tender lips of her pussy. When he licked her she jerked uncontrollably, reached down to grab his head, but not to pull it away. She held him there while saying, "Jesus, what the hell are you doin'?"

He couldn't answer because his face was pressed rightly to her, and his mouth was working avidly. Eventually her legs began to tremble, and then her belly. But before the tremors could run through her entire body he stopped and quickly mounted her. He grabbed her ankles and spread her, drove himself into her, and took her the rest of the way by fucking her as hard and as fast as he could . . .

"Jesus Christ!" she said later. "You got your friend's stamina, but you smell better than he did, and you know more nasty stuff than he did. All he wanted to do was rut, but you . . . I been a whore a long time, but I ain't never had a man do some of the things you done to me."

He was lying on his back, trying to get his own breath back.

"You wore me out," he said finally.

"I wore you out?" she asked. "God, I ain't gonna be able to walk straight tomorrow."

"Well then," he said, "maybe we gave each other something to remember each other by."

"I'd say so," she said, "but we ain't done, are we?" Her hand came over and crept down his belly until she held his cock in her hand. She stroked it, and it began to swell in her palm.

"Jesus, lady . . ."

"Naw," she said, "you ain't done at all, are ya?"

She rolled over, slid down and pressed her face to his burgeoning cock.

"You're not going to get much out of me, Angie . . . oooh . . ."

She took his penis into her mouth and began to suck him, proving him wrong.

SEVEN

Angie stayed the night.

Clint woke the next morning with Angie lying halfway across him. The weight of her breasts was not at all unpleasant, but she was snoring, and that was pretty unladylike.

He slid gently from beneath her, so as not to wake her. He wanted to get some breakfast and get on the trail, and if he woke her he knew what would happen: He wouldn't get out of that room 'til noon.

He dressed quickly and quietly and slipped from the room while Angie snored on.

He stopped into the restaurant, where a few early risers were already having breakfast, including the bartender from the White Wolf Saloon.

"Hey, Mr. Adams," he said. "Come and join me."

Clint decided, why not? Maybe the young man had

remembered something about Jesse Trapp that had eluded him the day before.

Clint walked over and sat down opposite the bartender and ordered steak and eggs when the waiter came over.

"Why don't we start with your name?" Clint asked, pouring himself some weak coffee. "I never did hear it."

"Oh, sorry," the man said. "My name's Eddie Reade."

"So, Eddie, you remember anything else about Jesse Trapp? Maybe something else he said?"

"No, not really. Mostly he just told stories."

"And did you believe them all?"

"They were all entertaining," he said. "Most of the guys in the saloon enjoyed them . . ." A funny look came over his face as his voice trailed off.

"Something occur to you?" Clint asked.

"Well, one thing," Eddie said.

"What?"

"There was another man in the saloon, sitting alone. He seemed to be listening to your friend talk, but not for the same reasons the rest of us was."

"What do you mean?"

"I mean, he wasn't enjoying the tall tales the way we were," Eddie said. "But he was watching Trapp. At one point, he came up to the bar to get another beer. I seen him stand behind Trapp and sort of . . . measure him."

"Taking his measure, you mean?"

"Yeah, like that."

"What'd the man look like?"

"I don't know," Eddie said with a shrug. "Thirties, tall, but not as tall as you. Thicker than you, though."

The waiter came with Clint's breakfast, set it in front of him. Clint ate while they continued to talk.

"You think he was following him?"

"No," Eddie said. "He got there before Trapp."

"So he was waiting for him?"

"No," Eddie said, shaking his head. "More like he got interested in him when he walked in."

Clint thought about it for a moment.

"Do you think maybe he recognized him when he walked in?"

"Could be."

"Did he follow him when he left?"

"When Trapp left, he left with the sheriff," Eddie said. "No, the other man stayed. He left later."

"Did you see him again?"

"I didn't see either of them again."

Clint ate in silence for a while. Whether the man recognized Trapp or developed an interest in him, maybe he'd followed Jesse when he left.

"You leavin' today?" Eddie asked.

"As soon as I finish this."

"Didn't get to hear any stories from you."

"I don't tell stories," Clint said. "You'll have to survive a while on the ones Jesse told you."

He ate the rest of his breakfast in silence, and then went to the livery.

"Sure, I remember," the liveryman said. "Great big smelly fella."

"That's right. Which stall was his horse in?"

"That one there." The man pointed.

"Any horses been in there since?"

"Nope."

"What was he riding?"

"A big gray—not as big as yours, but a good mount."

Clint walked over to have a look. From the tracks, he could see that the horse was very large. But he needed something more to identify the tracks for him. He took a good closer look and found a cut in the front left hoof. Nothing to make the horse lame, but just enough for him to identify the tracks. It was what he needed to be able to follow Jesse.

"Okay, thanks."

"Takin' your horse?"

"Yep," Clint said. "Leavin' today."

"Too bad," the man said. "That's a fine animal."

Clint saddled Eclipse and walked him out, then mounted up. The liveryman came out to watch him ride away.

"Do you always do that?" Clint asked.

"Do what?"

"Come out to watch your customers ride off?"

The man scratched his head.

"Ya know, I been doin' this job for over forty years," he said, "one place or another. But . . . yeah, I think I do."

"Which way did the man on the big gray go?"

The man thought a moment then said, "North."

"Thanks."

"And so did the other man."

"The other man?" Clint turned Eclipse back to the liveryman. "What other man?"

"The one who left soon after your friend."

"What'd he look like?"

"Thirties, kinda thick, not as tall as you."

"And he rode in the same direction?"

"Yup."

"Did he say anything?"

"Nope. Neither of them did. They just . . . left."

"What's the other man riding?"

"A mustang. Small, but nice. It could probably outlast that big gray, but not your horse."

"Anything else you can tell me?"

The man shrugged.

"Your friend carried a big buffalo gun," he said. "Other fella a Winchester, and a sidearm. That's about it."

"Okay," Clint said. "Thanks."

"Good luck to you."

Clint turned Eclipse, and rode north.

EIGHT

Jesse Trapp loved being in the saddle, especially since he'd started riding this big gray. He'd had the horse about five months now. He'd never named his mount before because he never knew when he'd have to eat his horse. Why name something you may some day have to eat. He hadn't named this one, either, but he tended to think of him as Big Gray.

"You and me, Big Gray," he said, "we're gonna make us some money up in Montana. They got them a wolf that's hard to kill. Best kind, I say. Maybe give us a run for our money, eh?" He patted the horse's neck.

He turned and looked behind him. Although he saw nothing, he had the feeling someone—or something—was there.

"Reckon they'll show themselves, eventually," he said. "Got us a town up ahead bigger than that last one. We'll restock there, get you some good feed, and me a decent steak. 'Bout the only thing that last town had was a decent whore. Oh yeah, and some fellers who liked a good tale."

But now, Montana, and a white wolf.

The man trailing Jesse Trapp was named Cole West. Since John Henry Trapp had killed two of his brothers several years ago just because they were looting some of his traps, Cole West was determined to exact his own brand of revenge—or justice, depending on how you looked at things.

He didn't want to kill John Henry outright, even if he had been able to find him. Cole West was a patient man, though. He'd been waiting years for an opportunity to present itself, and here it was. John Henry Trapp's brother walked into his life, and into his sights.

All he had to do was track him, and wait for the right moment.

When Clint cleared Little Town he examined the ground, found Jesse Trapp's tracks, and began to follow them. Along the way he managed to locate the trailing tracks, as well. One man, probably tracking Jesse rather than following him. And probably with bad intentions.

Jesse was the youngest of the seven Trapp brothers. He was also one of only two who were still alive. John Henry had spent over twenty years in prison. During that time, five of his brothers had met their maker. Two had been killed by animals—a bear, and a big cat—one was killed by Indians, one by a group of hunters (all of whom went to prison for the crime) and the fifth one had been tracked down and killed by a bounty hunter.

John Henry was the oldest of them all. When he got out of jail, John Henry had gone back to the Rockies, after he found and killed the men who had killed his wife all those years ago. He was in the Rockies now, where the law couldn't find him, where bounty hunters still hunted for him, where his legend continued to grow.

Jesse wasn't a legend, but he had as reputation as a brawler, a tracker, and a hunter. His specialty was hunting rogue animals—bears, cats, and wolves that got a taste of blood—animal or human—and would stop at nothing to satisfy it.

Clint had hunted with Jesse twice, had managed to hold his own. He'd also hunted with John Henry once, in the mountains. He'd hunted for animals with Jesse, for men with John Henry. He considered both men friends.

But John Henry was far from where they were going now. If Jesse needed help, it would come from Clint Adams.

Jesse Trapp rode into the town of Greybull, a town considerably larger than Little Town had been. He'd been there before on previous rides to Montana. He reined in Big Gray in front of the general store, dismounted, and entered, still wearing his buffalo skins. The people inside immediately noticed the smell.

"I'd know that smell anywhere," said Arlo Krupp, the owner. "That you, you old reprobate?"

"It's me," Jesse said, "but I don't know what no repro-whatsit is."

"Come on over here, Jesse."

Two women and a man left the store while Jesse approached the counter. The two men shook hands warmly.

"Sorry to cost you some customers."

"They weren't gonna buy anythin', anyway," Krupp said. "Whaddaya up to?"

"Montana," Jesse said. "They got them a rogue white wolf up there."

"A white?" Krupp asked. "I thought there was no such thing as a true white?"

"That's what some folks say," Jesse replied. "Me, when I see a white wolf, I see a white wolf."

"So whaddaya need?"

"To get outfitted," Jesse said, "for a hunt."

"Well, okay," Krupp said. "Let's get started.

NINE

Cole West rode into Greybull, Wyoming, and saw Jesse Trapp's big gray still tied off outside the general store.

He could have waited outside and picked Trapp off with his rifle when he came out, but that wouldn't satisfy him. He wanted to see Trapp's face when he told him who he was and why he was dying.

He had seen the telegraph office when he rode in. It was a block back, so he turned his horse and rode back to it. He was only about an hour behind Trapp, and if the man was getting outfitted it would take a while.

He had time to send an important telegram and then continue tracking the man.

Trapp looked at the pile of items on the counter in front of Krupp, who was using a stubby pencil to figure out the cost. The man's gray hair was nearly standing up on end as he frowned at the numbers and licked the end of the pencil.

"Ammunition . . . you're lucky I still carry fifth-caliber . . . flour, salt, coffee, beans, beef jerky, bacon . . ."

Krupp kept reading off items and adding them up. Trapp was glad he had requested an advance on his fee.

"Have you heard from John Henry?" Krupp asked.

"Not for a long time."

"Have you tried?"

"I don't have to try," Jesse said. "I know where to find him. I just ain't needed to."

"Not for this hunt?"

"I got somebody else in mind," Jesse said. "I was supposed to meet up with him, but I'll bet he's trailin' along behind me. If you see him, let him know I'm heading north."

"Where in Montana?"

"A place called Wolf Creek."

"How very fittin'," Krupp said. "Here's your bill, old friend."

Jesse said, "You know I can't read, you old pirate. Tell me how much you're overcharging me."

He did.

"See? You're a pirate."

"I'm givin' you the friendly rate," Krupp said, laughing.

"Yeah, yeah." Jesse took out his money. He couldn't read, but he could count. He laid bills into Krupp's open hand as the man smiled at him.

"You got a pack mule?"

"No," Jesse said. "I thought I'd get one here. No point in draggin' it all across Wyoming."

"Good point. I've got a few out back. Wanna have a look?"

"Lead the way. Better to buy one from a friend, even if he is a pirate."

"I was a pirate, Jesse," Krupp said, "but that was many years ago, when I was at sea. Now I'm just a merchant. Come on."

Cole waited for a reply to his telegraph. He stood outside the office. From there he could look down the street and see the gray in front of the general store. Trapp was still inside.

He'd actually sent three telegrams, and expected to hear back from all three. The men he was putting out a call to would respond immediately. And they would come, to wherever he asked them to.

"Hey, mister?" the clerk called

Cole stuck his head back inside. "Yeah?"

"First answer's here."

He went inside to retrieve it. "Two more to come," he said.

"What if they don't?"

"They will," Cole said. "I'll be outside."

He stepped back onto the boardwalk and read the reply: ONE MAN ON HIS WAY; TWO TO COME.

"The old one," Trapp said, pointing.

"Why not the young one?"

"'Cause I'll be able depend on the old one more," Jesse said. "You oughta know that."

"Well, okay," Krupp said. "Suit yerself. I'll write you up a bill."

"Goddammit, I can't read the damn thing, so just tell me how much."

"Come back inside," Krupp said.

"I'll walk the mule around to the front and meet you there," Trapp said.

"Suit yerself," Krupp said again.

By the time Trapp and Krupp had the pack mule loaded, Cole had the three telegrams in his pocket. All three men had agreed to meet him in Montana. He didn't know where Trapp was heading, but if they kept going north he'd be able to meet up with his three friends.

Cole felt no shame over asking three other men to help him kill Trapp. No shame at all. In the end, the important thing was to kill Trapp. Didn't matter how it got done.

Didn't matter at all.

Trapp checked the lines on the mule, made sure the supplies were tied down tight.

"You gonna stay the night in town?" Krupp asked.

"No," Trapp said. "I'll get started and maybe camp three or four hours out."

"What about that feller you said is comin' to help ya?" Krupp asked. "You wanna tell me his name so I know who I'm waitin' fer?"

Trapp mounted his gray and said, "Sure. His name's Clint Adams."

As Trapp rode off Krupp said, "Ya don't say."

TEN

It was almost dark by the time Clint rode into Greybull.

He was still following Jesse Trapp's trail, but there was no point trying to do that at night.

He saw to Eclipse's comforts, then got himself a room at one of the hotels. After that he went to the saloon for a beer.

As the bartender served it, he asked if there had been any sign of Jesse Trapp in town.

"Big fella, smelly buffalo skins," Clint said. "You'd remember him."

"I guess I would, but I didn't see nobody fittin' that description in here, or in town."

"Okay, thanks."

He nursed his beer, talked to a couple more men about whether or not they'd seen a big man in smelly skins. No luck.

He ordered a second beer and while he was waiting for it another man came up next to him. He was a skinny fellow with lots of gray hair sticking out from beneath a captain's cap.

"Heard you're askin' questions about a big fella in some smelly skins."

"That's right."

"Would that be Jesse Trapp you're lookin' for?"

"That's right." Clint turned and looked at him. "You know Jesse?"

"I do."

"How about a beer?"

"Well, sure. Thanks."

Clint waved at the bartender for another beer.

"What's your name?" Clint asked, passing a beer over to the man.

"I'm Arlo Krupp."

"What's your business, Mr. Krupp?"

"I own the general store."

"How do you know Jesse Trapp?"

"Fact is, I know Jesse and his brother, John Henry— though I ain't seen John in years."

"And Jesse?"

"Fact is, he was in here two days ago, gettin' himself outfitted for a hunt."

"He say where he was going for this hunt?"

"He said he was gonna be joined by a friend of his, Clint Adams," Krupp said. "Would that be you?"

"It would."

"Well, I'll be . . . I almost didn't believe him when he told me."

"What exactly did he tell you?"

"That he was goin' to Montana to hunt some white

wolf that's gone rogue. And that he asked you to meet up with him and help him out."

"Well, that much is true," Clint said. "I was supposed to meet him in a place called Little Town, but I got there late."

"Yeah, them Trapps," Krupp said, "they're nothin' if they ain't impatient. You say you're gonna meet up with them somewheres, you better be there."

"I know that," Clint said. "He outfit completely?"

"Oh yeah," Krupp said, "he figured to ride into Montana all set for huntin'."

"That mean a pack animal?"

Krupp nodded.

"Bought a mule off me, along with everythin' else," Krupp said.

"So he'll be traveling even slower than he was," Clint said.

"That's a fact," Krupp said. "You oughta be able to catch up with him pretty quick."

"He say anything about anyone else tracking him?" Clint asked.

"No, why?"

"Well, I've been following his trail a few days since Little Town. Seems to me somebody else is doing the same thing."

"Naw, he didn't say nothin' about nobody else," Krupp said. "Maybe he didn't notice."

"A man like Jesse should notice something like that," Clint said. "Unless he's past it."

"If he's past it," Krupp said, "maybe that wolf'll get 'im."

"Maybe," Clint said, "but not if I can help it."

"You stayin' the night, Mr. Adams?"

Clint nodded. "Figure I can catch up to him in the daylight," Clint said. "Won't be able to see his trail at night."

"Maybe you don't have to follow his trail," Krupp said.

"What do you mean?"

"Well, maybe I know where he's goin' on this wolf hunt."

Clint studied the man briefly, then said, "Bartender, another beer for my friend."

ELEVEN

Toting a pack mule all over creation was a pain in the ass.

Jesse usually traveled without a pack animal. He preferred not having to load it and unload it every night and every morning. But on a hunt like this the animal would be necessary. When he got where he was going, when the hunt began, he'd have to stay on the wolf's trail until he got it.

He was camped one night into Montana. He could feel the difference in the air—it had a cold bite to it, which he liked. His fire kept him warm enough, but the cold kept the night clear and he could see all the stars in the heavens. This was the only kind of roof he and his brother ever wanted to live under.

He took the coffeepot off the stove and poured himself a cup, scooped some beans right out of the pan, and ate them. He looked over at his horse and the mule, standing side-by-side. They seemed to be getting along just fine.

He looked out into the dark, his night vision allowing him to see just fine. If there was somebody out there, he'd either see him or hear him coming in. If he was a piece away, maybe at his own fire, he didn't care. The only thing that concerned him was if someone was out in the dark with a rifle, taking a bead on him. Usually, though, when he was under somebody's gun barrel or in his sights, he could feel it, and tonight he felt nothing. The big fella usually raised a fuss if man or animal tried to come near the camp.

He finished his dinner, then rolled up in his bedroll to get some shut-eye.

Cole West made his own camp, a mile behind Trapp. He was downwind of the man, so while he could smell Trapp's fire, Trapp couldn't smell his.

Cole made some coffee, then made a meal out of beef jerky. It suited him. He'd learned to eat light on the trail. It made a steak dinner that much more special when you got to town.

He thought about Trapp, camped up ahead. He might have been able to sneak up on him while he was sleeping— if he was sleeping. But he'd already sent for help, so he figured he might as well wait for the three men to meet up with him.

He finished eating, made sure the fire would stay lit by adding more wood, then rolled himself up in his bed-roll and went to sleep.

Even farther back, Clint camped for the night. He had no reason to worry about anyone smelling his fire, but he also traveled light. He carried a coffeepot and some coffee, and Krupp had sold him some canned peaches. He wasn't carrying a frying pan this time around, so there was no use in bringing beans or bacon. He made a meal out of the coffee and peaches.

He could smell somebody's fire up ahead of him. He didn't know if it was Trapp's or if it belonged to the man following him. It didn't much matter, though. He'd be catching up with Trapp well before he got to Wolf Creek. Might even first run across the man who was trailing Trapp. Unless the man was good enough to avoid him.

He had some more coffee, walked to the edge of the light cast by his fire, and stared into the darkness while he finished it.

When he was done he returned to the fire, wrapped a blanket around himself, and laid down with his gun by his head.

TWELVE

Cole West knew somebody was behind him. What he didn't know was what they wanted. Were they tracking, or just drifting?

He decided not to find out. He took cover behind some rocks, dismounted, wiped away his tracks, then kept his horse quiet and waited. Eventually, a rider came along, riding at a decent pace. The man was astride a big horse, an Arabian if he wasn't wrong. Didn't see many of those in the West. They usually weren't very sure-footed, although they did have a lot of stamina.

The man had his head down, looking at the ground, so he was following a trail. His, or Trapp's? No way of telling. Or was there? If the man was any good at tracking he'd know that Cole had wiped his tracks. Cole continued to watch the rider closely for his reaction.

Clint reined Eclipse in and stared at the ground. Someone had taken steps to cover their tracks, but whoever it was hadn't wiped out any of Trapp's. A person had to be real careful to do that, and knowledgeable.

Clint was careful not to look around. If the aim of whoever had covered his tracks was to kill him, he would have fired by now. If he looked around now and gave away the fact that he knew what was going on, the man might go ahead and fire anyway.

Clint gigged Eclipse into motion and allowed the big Darley Arabian to simply walk, as if nothing was unusual.

He continued to follow Trapp's trail, which was now the only one.

Cole West watched Clint Adams closely, prepared to fire if he had to. He didn't. The man never looked around, just continued forward. Cole waited until there was no space between them, then rode out of his hiding place and continued to follow the tracks of Jesse Trapp and, now, Clint Adams.

Trapp camped that night, knowing that he was about two days out of Wolf Creek. He'd skirt Helena. It was a big town, but there was no reason to stop there. He was already properly outfitted and he had no need of a telegraph. If Clint Adams was going to catch up to him, he'd do it in the next two days—or not at all. If he didn't show, Trapp was prepared to track the wolf himself.

Darkness fell and Clint kept riding. The moon was bright enough for him to see, and he wanted to catch up to Trapp while the man was camped.

When the smell of coffee made its way to his nostrils he knew he was close. And then, suddenly, he saw the light ahead.

A fire.

He rode for it.

Trapp heard somebody coming in the darkness. He grabbed his Big Fifty and laid it across his thighs. Stared out into the dark.

"Hello, the camp!" came a voice.

A familiar voice.

"Clint, goddammit, is that you?" Trapp called.

"It's me, Jesse."

"Well, come ahead," Trapp said, still holding his rifle on his knees. "I won't blow your head off."

He waited for Clint to ride into his camp.

Clint could see Trapp sitting by the fire, rifle across his knees. He rode Eclipse into the light.

"Well, that ain't Duke," Trapp said, standing up.

"Had to put Duke out to pasture," Clint said. "This is Eclipse."

"Almost as fine-lookin' an animal as Duke," Trapp said. "How do you manage it?"

"This one was a gift."

"Well, come ahead," Trapp said, letting the barrel of the big buffalo gun point downward. "I got coffee, and I can put on some beans."

"Sounds good."

Clint dismounted, shook hands with the big hunter, then set about unsaddling Eclipse while Trapp cooked the beans.

When Clint returned to the fire, Trapp handed him a cup of coffee. It was good and strong, and warmed Clint's innards immediately. It may have been fall, but this was Montana, and it was cold.

"Thanks."

"I remember you like it strong."

Clint sat down and Jesse doled out the beans, leaving the pan empty.

"You know you've got a tail?" Clint asked.

"I thought it might be you."

"There was somebody between you and me."

"Was?"

"He changed places with me," Clint said. "Rubbed out his tracks, but I noticed."

"You was always pretty good following signs."

"Not as good as you and John Henry."

"You seen big John lately?" Jesse asked.

"Not in years."

"Yeah, me neither," Trapp said. "You didn't get a look at whoever it was?"

"No."

"And you think he's still behind us?"

"Oh, yeah."

"Should we take 'im?"

"You got any idea who it might be?"

"No."

"Somebody with a grudge."

"There's lot of folks with a grudge."

"And you didn't see anyone when you were in Little Town?" Clint asked. "The bartender told me the man was in the saloon with you?"

"Was he? I was busy drinkin' and tellin' tales."

"And he was listening."

"Huh. Maybe I'm gettin' old."

"Whether or not we take him is up to you."

"If he was gonna shoot from cover, he's had his chances."

"With both of us."

"Let's just keep goin', then," Trapp said. "I wanna get to Wolf Creek as soon as we can."

"Fine with me," Clint said. "Were you going to stop in Helena?"

"No, jus' keep goin'."

"Also fine with me," Clint said. "These beans are good."

"I put some molasses in 'em."

"Maybe," Clint said, "while we're eating, you can tell me what we're going to be dealing with once we get to Wolf Creek?"

Trapp shrugged and said, "I'll tell ya what I know."

THIRTEEN

"I got a telegram about a rogue white up in Wolf Creek. First it was killin' stock, and then people. They ain't been able to track it down, let alone kill it."

"When's the last time you hunted a white?"

"Been a while," Jesse admitted.

"What have you been doing?"

"Hunting," Jesse said. "I got me some bears, some big cats, but a wolf—and a white wolf—that's the biggest challenge. They're cunning."

"I've hunted wolves," Clint said, "but never a white. Why'd you ask me along?"

"A white might be leading a pack," Jesse said. "If this one is, I'll need help."

"Why not John Henry?"

"He comes down from his mountain, he'll have a target on his back," Jesse said. "He still has a price on his head. I'd rather he stays where he is. That left you. Ain't nobody else I can count on."

"Well, I'm flattered."

"Don't be," Jesse Trapp said. "I ain't tryin' to flatter you. I'm tryin' to stay alive."

"I understand."

"We better set a watch for tonight, in case our friend decides to try somethin'," Jesse suggested.

"I'll go first," Clint said. "I want to have more coffee."

"Suits me," Jesse said.

Jesse laid down and wrapped himself in his smelly skins.

"Jesse, you ever consider getting yourself some new skins?"

"Why?" Jesse asked. "I just got these broke in."

"Yeah, but they smell."

"Wait until you get cold enough," Jesse warned him. "Then you'll wish you had you some of these here smelly skins."

Lint could already feel the chill creeping into his bones.

"Yeah," he said, "you're probably right."

Jesse didn't say anything else, and within moments Clint could hear him snoring.

About a mile behind them, Cole West had already retired and was also snoring contentedly.

FOURTEEN

Clint woke shivering.

Jesse was sitting by the fire wrapped in his skins, drinking coffee. He looked comfortable.

"Got to get me some skins," Clint said, coming up to the fire.

"Toldja," Jesse said, holding a cup of coffee out to him.

"Thanks." He sat across the fire from Jesse.

"You want some breakfast?" Jesse asked. "I can fry up some bacon."

"No, I'm good," Clint said. "Coffee's enough. I think we should get moving."

"I think so, too," Jesse said. "You get the fire, I'll get the horses."

"Not my horse," Clint said. "He'll take a piece out of you."

"Naw," Jesse said, "horses love me. Don't worry."

"Your funeral."

Clint poured some more coffee into his cup, then emptied the rest of it on the fire. He had to kick dirt on it to get it completely doused.

He was surprised when Jesse Trapp walked Eclipse over to him, calm and saddled.

"I don't believe it," he said, taking the reins.

"Yeah, well," Jesse said, holding up his left hand, "you weren't all wrong." There was a bloody gash on his hand where Eclipse had nipped him. "But after that we got along."

Jesse patted the big horse's neck to illustrate his point. Eclipse suffered the touch impassively.

Clint looked at Jesse's gray. He was almost as big as Eclipse.

"Good horse," he said.

"Best one I've ever had, I think."

"Name him?"

"Naw."

"Come on."

"I just think of him as Big Gray."

"There you go."

"I'll need help with the mule," Jesse said. "He's a little ornery this morning."

"Sure."

They walked to the mule. Clint held the animal's head and talked to him while Jesse loaded him down, then Clint helped to tie down the mule's load.

"He's got some age on him," Clint said.

"Ain't we all?" Jesse replied.

Once they had the mule packed they walked him over to where the horses were and mounted up.

"We cover some miles today we can make Wolf Creek before dark tomorrow."

"I'm willing," Clint said. "Let's push it. Maybe it'll test whoever's on our tail."

"Let's go, then."

With a second man riding with him, Jesse Trapp was now leaving an easier trail to follow. For that reason Cole knew he could detour to Helena and meet his men without losing them.

He rode into Helena at midday and went right to a saloon called the Second Chance Saloon.

"There he is," Dave Willis said as Cole came into the saloon.

Willis, Harve Shoemaker, and Randy Truett all stood up as Cole reached them.

"Thanks for comin'," Cole said, shaking hands with all three.

"Where is he?" Willis asked. "Where's Trapp?"

"He's headin' north through Montana."

"That's all you know?" Shoemaker asked.

"No," Cole said. "I've been trailin' him. He's leavin' a trail that's easy to follow. He's got a mule and a second man with him. I broke off to meet you fellas. Now we'll pick up the trail again."

"Is he headin' to his brother?" Truett asked. "I'd really like a crack at John Henry."

"No," Cole said, "I don't think so. He's on his way to hunt for a wolf. I think John Henry is still in the Rockies somewhere."

"So all we get is the brother?" Willis asked.

"We all know what kind of man John Henry is," Cole said. "Once he hears that we killed Jesse, he'll come down from his mountain."

"And then we'll have him," Shoemaker said.

"That's right."

"Then what are we waitin' for?" Truett asked. "Let's pick up his trail."

"All we gotta do is head north out of town, and then west. We'll pick it up."

"What about an outfit?"

"Just what we can carry in our saddlebags," Cole said. "Some coffee and a coffeepot, beef jerky, a frying pan, some beans and bacon, some shells. We'll split it all up."

"We buyin' it?" Shoemaker asked. "Or takin' it?"

"We'll buy it," Cole said. "I don't wanna attract any attention. No trouble. Okay, boys?"

"Okay," Shoemaker said.

"Yeah, good," Truett said.

"You sure about this?" Willis asked.

"Yeah, Dave," Cole West said, "I'm sure. This is the way it's gotta be."

"Okay," Willis said. "Yeah, okay. Let's buy the stuff and get goin'."

"I passed the general store on the way here," Cole said, "Dave and me go inside, you boys stay outside with the horses. Then we'll load the stuff and get movin.'"

The others all nodded.

"And no trouble, right?"

The other three nodded, and Dave Willis said, "Right."

FIFTEEN

Clint Adams and Jesse Trapp left Helena behind them and headed directly north for Wolf Creek. They talked for a while during the ride, catching up on the years that had passed since they last saw each other. Eventually, they ran out of conversation and rode in silence.

The men made one stop to eat beef jerky and drank water. They didn't rest for very long, though, because they wanted to cover a lot of miles. Both of their horses and the mule had the stamina to be pushed.

They moved on.

The four riders left Helena, rode north, and picked up the trail being left by two horses and a mule.

"See?" Cole said, pointing at the tracks.

"How do we know it's them?" Willis asked.

"Two horses and a mule," Cole said.

"How do you know one of those tracks is bein' left by a mule?" Shoemaker asked.

"You never could track worth a damn, Shoe," Truett said, laughing.

"Yeah, like you know a mule track from a horse's," Shoemaker said.

"Yeah, well . . ." Truett said.

"Mules tracks are smaller and narrower," Cole said. "See?"

"We don't have to see," Willis said. "As long as you do, Cole."

"Let's follow 'em, and take our time," Cole said.

"Why? If we push it, we can run them down," Shoemaker said.

"I wanna let them get where they're goin'," Cole said. "Get settled in. Think all they gotta worry about is a wolf."

"And then we move," Willis said. "I like it."

"I ain't got the patience you fellas got," Truett said.

"Me, neither," Shoemaker said, "but it's your call, Cole."

"That's right, it is," Cole said.

Willis looked ahead at the sky and said, "Looks like we're gonna get some fall snow up ahead."

"Might make it hard for Trapp to hunt a white wolf," Shoemaker said.

"Probably right," Cole said, "but I ain't about to let any wolf beat me to Jesse Trapp, even if I gotta kill the animal myself."

"Snow," Trapp said. "Sittin' heavy in those clouds up ahead."

"Probably hanging right over Wolf Creek," Clint said. "Bad luck."

"That'll just add to the challenge," Trapp said.

"I don't find hunting a killer wolf a challenge, Jesse," Clint said. "I find it a chore."

"I understand that," Jesse said. "Me and John Henry, we like matching wits with these animals, especially a wolf—and a white wolf, to boot."

They rode along talking white wolves. Or rather, Jesse talked, and Clint listened.

"It's odd to find a single white wolf doin' this kind of damage," he said. "Like all wolves, they usually hunt in packs."

"Don't usually see them in Montana, do you?"

"No," Jesse said. "Usually in Alaska or Canada. They like the cold, and it's odd for them to come south, where it's not as cold."

"It's going to be cold here, though," Clint said. "Especially if we're getting snow."

"They like it frigid," Jesse said. "They grow an extra coat when it's real cold."

"Tell me more about them," Clint said. "If I'm going to hunt one, I want to know as much as I can."

"They have sharp eyesight, a keen sense of smell and hearing. All of that helps make them great hunters. Oh yeah, they have forty-two teeth."

"Forty-two?" Clint asked. "How do you know that?"

"I counted."

"Why would you do that?"

"Like you just said," Jesse replied, "ya gotta know

everything about your prey when you're hunting. Don't matter if it's man or beast."

"Speaking of man," Clint said, "I'm not feeling our tail anymore."

"Maybe he gave up," Jesse said.

"Yeah, maybe," Clint said.

"You don't think so?"

"I'm thinking about how close we came to Helena."

"And?"

"He could have diverted to Helena, got some help, figured he could easily pick up our trail again. With two horses and a mule, we aren't exactly hard to track."

"Help, huh?"

"Well, I'm figuring he's seen me and knows I'm with you."

"Does he know who you are?"

"I don't know," Clint said. "I guess he would have had to recognize me."

"So maybe he don't know who you are," Jesse said. "Maybe he just thinks I got another man with me, but not the Gunsmith. So we got surprise on our side."

"I'd rather not," Clint said. "Bad enough we've got to deal with a wolf. I don't want to have to deal with two, three, maybe more men coming up on us."

"Well," Jesse said, "I'll leave that to you. My part is trackin' the wolf. Your part is watchin' for the men."

"I thought my part was backing you in case there's more than one wolf."

"Well," Jesse Trapp said, "we'll just have to back each other."

"That's what being partners is all about," Clint replied.

SIXTEEN

It got colder as they moved farther north. By the time they made camp it had started to snow. Clint could see what Jesse meant about the skins. Smelly or not, they were keeping Jesse warm. Clint felt a chill right down to his bones.

"When did you kill that buffalo you're wearing?" he asked over the fire.

"Many years ago."

"You wouldn't happen to have another one hanging around, would you?"

"Nope," Jesse said. "This is my only one. Do you have another shirt in your saddlebags?"

"A couple."

"My advice is to put them on, then put your jacket back on. You should have brought a heavier coat."

"Maybe I can buy one when we get to Wolf Creek."

"There's a store in Marysville," Jesse said, "but it's a few miles out of our way."

"That's okay," Clint said. "I'll wait 'til we get to Wolf's Creek. Meanwhile, I'll just get those other shirts."

"You might want to get your horse's blanket, too," Jesse said. "Believe me, you won't mind the smell."

Later, wearing two shirts, his jacket, and wrapped in the horse blanket, he found he didn't mind the smell.

It wasn't snowing where Cole West camped with his three partners.

"Why can't we keep goin'?" an impatient Shoemaker asked.

"I'm not takin' a chance on my horse breakin' a leg in the dark just to satisfy you, Shoe," Cole said.

"Me, neither," Truett said. "It's like Cole says, we'll catch 'em. There's no hurry."

Shoemaker looked to Willis for support, but the man just drank his coffee and ate his beans.

"Shut up and eat, Shoe," Cole said.

"That ain't no way to talk to me," Shoemaker said. "I come all this way to help you."

"Yeah, you did," Cole said, "and I appreciate it, but if you don't keep quiet I'm gonna have to shoot you."

Shoemaker grumbled under his breath, and ate.

Jesse took the first watch, drank a whole pot of coffee while he did, then made a fresh pot before he went to wake Clint up.

"Anything?" Clint asked, getting to his feet.

"Ain't seen or heard a thing," Jesse said, settling down on his bedroll. "I made ya a fresh pot of coffee."

"Much obliged, Jesse."

Clint took his horse blanket to the fire, wrapped it around himself, and sat down. He poured himself a cup of coffee and enjoyed the way it warmed his hands, then his throat and his belly.

He figured whoever was on their trail had camped far enough away so their fire couldn't be seen. They were downwind so they didn't have to worry about the smells of their camp reaching Clint and Jesse.

Clint figured the man trailing Jesse had to be pretty smart. He'd stayed out of sight, had probably gotten himself some help, made sure Clint hadn't spotted him while actually letting him get by. And he'd managed to resist taking a shot at Clint, which was smart. Clint was not his main concern. That was Jesse Trapp. Clint wondered, when he and Jesse finally caught the man, what his gripe would turn out to be.

SEVENTEEN

By midday the next day they'd made it to Wolf Creek.

Before they arrived, Caleb Farnsworth rode into town with a few of his boys and stopped at the Wayfarer's Saloon.

"Set 'em up for my boys," he told the bartender. "Beer, no whiskey."

The bartender drew four beers and set them in front of Farnsworth and his men.

"Any luck, Mr. Farnsworth?" he asked.

"No," Farnsworth said.

"That wolf's gotta be the devil himself," Lee Thompson said. "We'd catch his trail, track him a while, and then suddenly . . . gone. Just like that. Like he just lifted up in the air."

"Shut up, Lee," Farnsworth said. "It's just a damn wolf."

"Sure, boss."

The four men, dog tired from a fruitless hunt, hung their heads over their beer mugs.

Over in one corner sat Evangeline Parkins, alone at a table with a beer of her own. She was the only woman in town who ever went into the Wayfarer's, and the only one they'd let into the saloon. Actually, they let her in because if they didn't she'd probably kick their rumps. The only other women in the place were two girls working the saloon floor.

She saw Farnsworth and his boys come in and waited 'til they were set up at the bar. Once they were, she picked up her beer and walked over.

"Mr. Farnsworth," she said, sidling up next to him.

Farnsworth looked at her and then rolled his eyes.

"Evangeline."

"No luck catchin' that wolf, huh?"

"No, no luck," he said. "We caught sight of his trail a time or two, but no luck in trackin' him down."

"Never even got a shot at him?" she asked.

"Never even got a whiff."

"Well," she said, "I told you I'd kill it for you. All you got to do is hire me."

"Ain't no woman gonna catch that devil," Lee Thompson said. "No sir."

"That's for sure," Emmett Dexter said, laughing. "But then, Evangeline ain't exactly a woman, is she?"

"You shut your mouth, Emmett," Evangeline said. "I'm more woman than you'd ever be able to handle."

"How's a fella supposed to know that?" Dexter asked. "Can't see nothin' under all that dirt and those skins."

She decided to ignore him and looked at Farnsworth again.

"Whaddaya got to lose, Mr. Farnsworth?" she asked.

"Evangeline, I've hired a real wolf hunter. He'll be here any day now. If he wants you to go out with him, that's fine. Maybe he'll even pay you to back him up. But I am not gonna pay a woman to go out there and get herself torn apart by a wolf. No sir."

"I can take care of myself, Mr. Farnsworth."

"Yeah, maybe you can," he said. "But I ain't gonna have your death on my conscience, Evangeline. No sir."

"Mr. Farnsworth—"

"Come on, Evangeline," he said. "I'll buy you another beer if you'll just keep quiet and stop jawing at me."

Seeing she wasn't going to get what she wanted from him and said, "Yeah, okay, I'll take another beer."

He bought her a cold beer and she took it back to her corner table.

Clint and Jesse rode in, drawing some looks from the people on the street—probably because of the way Jesse looked in his skins, and the fully packed mule following along after them.

"What's the name of the man who sent for you?" Clint asked.

"Farnsworth," Jessie said, "Caleb Farnsworth. He's got a spread north of here, is losing his stock to the wolf, and had a man killed."

"Are we supposed to ride out to his place?"

"I suppose," Jesse said. "But I'd rather get us a couple of beers first, before we do that."

"And maybe a room," Clint said, "and a bath."

"A bath?" Jesse said, appalled. "Now that's just crazy talk!"

"Well," Clint said, "let's go to a saloon. Maybe they can give us directions out to the ranch."

EIGHTEEN

There was another saloon across the street from the Wayfarer's. Lee Thompson was staring out the window and saw the two men dismounting and going into the smaller saloon.

"Hey, boss?"

"Yeah, Lee?" Farnsworth said.

"Some fella wearing a whole bunch of buffalo skins just went into Rocky's saloon across the street," Thompson said. "You suppose that's your wolf hunter?"

"Might be," Farnsworth said, looking into his empty beer mug. "Maybe we better go on across and find out for sure, huh?"

Evangeline came running over as the four men pushed away from the bar.

"You mind if I tag along, Mr. Farnsworth?" she asked. "I wanna meet this great wolf hunter you sent for."

"Sure, Evangeline," he said, "you come ahead. We'll all go and meet him at the same time."

"Thanks."

Clint and Jesse Trapp were standing at the small bar having a beer when the batwings opened. Several men and a woman walked in. The woman was dressed similarly to Jesse, in skins, though hers weren't made from buffalo.

"Jesse Trapp?" one man asked.

Jesse turned to face them.

"That's right."

The spokesman extended his hand.

"Caleb Farnsworth."

Jesse shook the man's hand and said to Clint, "This is the man who sent for me. Mr. Farnsworth, this is my partner, Clint Adams."

"Clint Adams?" Farnsworth said.

"The Gunsmith?" one of the others said.

"I didn't know the Gunsmith was a wolfer," Lee Thompson said.

"I'm not," Clint said. "That's Jesse's talent. I'm just along as backup."

"Well," Farnsworth said, "we're glad to have the both of you here. My boys and I just came in from tryin' to track that animal for ten hours. We never got close."

"You shouldn't have done that," Jesse said. "If you been after him that long it's gonna make it harder for me to get close."

"We couldn't just sit around and let it kill more stock,

or men," Thompson said. "What if it starts goin' after women and children?"

"Keep your women and children inside," Jesse said.

"For how long?" one of the men asked.

"As long as the wolf is out there," Jesse said.

"Are you sure it's the same wolf?" Clint asked. "I mean, that the one that killed the stock is the same one that attacked the . . . man? Men? How many?"

"It's killed two men," Farnsworth said.

"What were the men doing?" Clint asked.

"One of them heard his horses in distress, went out to see what was wrong, and was attacked. He was torn apart," Farnsworth said.

"The second man was part of a party that was huntin' the wolf," Thompson said.

"Who are you?" Clint asked.

"Lee Thompson," the man said. "I work for Mr. Farnsworth."

"Okay, go ahead," Clint said.

"That's it. Four men were out huntin' the wolf. They split up and Herb Walter was killed."

"All right," Jesse said. "From this point on nobody hunts. Pass the word."

"We will," Farnsworth said.

"Mr. Farnsworth, we'll need just one man to show us the places where the wolf hit."

"I'll do it," Thompson said.

"Thompson knows all the spots," Farnsworth told them.

"Okay," Clint said. "Take the rest of the men and go home. The girl, too."

"I don't work for him," Evangeline said.

"Don't care who you work for, missy," Jesse said. "You got to get inside, where it's safe."

"I wanna hunt the wolf," she said. "I'm a good hunter."

Jesse looked at Farnsowrth.

"This is Evangeline Parkins. She lives around here."

"Miss Parkins," Clint said, "you better go home."

"I ain't," she said. "I'm gonna hunt that wolf with or without ya, so you might as well let me go with ya."

Clint and Jesse exchanged a look.

"I can shoot," she said. "Real good. And track. I'm a good hunter."

"You hunt them animals you're wearin'?" Jesse asked.

"Sure did."

"Those are wolf skins."

"Yup."

"Grays."

"Two of 'em," she said. "I killed 'em. Tracked 'em and killed 'em."

Jesse looked at Farnsworth.

"She's got experience," the man said. "Some."

"We should get settled," Clint said, "and then get started."

"Thompson will take you to the hotel," Farnsworth said. "They're holdin' one room, but you can have two. Take care of that, Lee."

"Yessir."

"When will you start?" Farnsworth asked.

"Your man can take us out in the mornin'," Jesse said. "I wanna see where the two men were killed."

"Okay," Farnsworth said. "Thompson'll be here early."

"What about me?" Evangeline asked. "Can I go?"

Jesse looked at her.

"You be here in the mornin', missy," he said. "You'll have breakfast with us."

"What's that mean?" she asked.

"If you can convince us that you have value," Clint said, "you can come."

Jesse pointed his finger at Farnsworth. "Keep the rest of your men home," he said. "And all the people in town and who live in the area. Everybody inside, or in town. Got it?"

"I got it," Farnsworth said.

"Who's the law in town?" Clint asked.

"We got a deputy," Farnsworth said.

"No sheriff?"

"I forget to tell you?" Farnsworth asked. "He was one of the men whom the wolf killed."

"Jesus," Clint said. "Okay, we'll probably have to talk to the deputy."

"I'll have him come and see you," Farnsworth promised.

Clint looked at Thompson.

"The hotel?"

"Follow me."

NINETEEN

Outside of town Cole, Willis, Shoemaker, and Truett stayed their horses and looked down on the town.

"They're in there," Shoemaker said.

"Yeah," Cole said.

"That mule slowed 'em down enough for us to catch up to them," Willis said. "We're only hours behind them."

"They're probably in a hotel bed," Truett said. "We can take 'em there."

"No," Cole said. "We'll take them outside. We got time."

"So what do we do?" Willis asked. "Camp out here in the cold while they're warm in a hotel bed?"

Cole looked at the three men.

"No," he said finally, "we're gonna be warm in some hotel beds, too."

"How we gonna do that?" Truett asked.

"You and Shoe ride in now, get yerselves a hotel room. If there's more than one hotel, you get a room in the first one you come to. Me and Willis will get a room in the next one."

"What if they see us?" Shoe asked.

"It don't matter," Cole said. "They don't know what you look like. They don't know what we look like."

"Four more strangers ridin' into town?" Willis asked. "They're gonna figure we're followin' them."

"It don't matter," Cole said. "They can't prove nothin'."

"And what are we gonna do then?" Truett asked. "Once we're in town."

"We're gonna watch 'em," Cole said. "We're gonna watch 'em real close."

Shoemaker and Truett rode into town while Cole and Willis continued to watch.

"What are we doin', Cole?"

"We're givin' 'em somethin' to think about," Cole said. "I want Jesse Trapp to wonder about it before he dies."

"And what if they come after us?"

"It's two to four," Cole said. "Don't worry about it, Dave."

TWENTY

At the hotel Clint got one room, Trapp another. They both stowed their gear and then met in the lobby. Thompson and Evangeline were still there, ignoring one another.

"We got to take care of the horses and the mule," Jesse said. "Then we could use a hot meal."

"There's a real good café down the street," Evangeline said. "I can take you there."

"No," Clint said, "Jesse and I will eat alone tonight. You eat with us tomorrow."

"What about me?" Thompson asked.

"Go home," Clint said. "Be back here tomorrow."

"Okay," Thompson said. "Okay."

They all stepped outside. The snow was starting to cover the ground.

"How bad could this get?" Clint asked.

"Bad," Thompson said.

"Real bad," Evangeline said.

"Great," Clint said.

* * *

Thompson went back to the Farnsworth ranch for the night. He'd be back in the morning.

Clint had to convince Evangeline to go home, and promised that they wouldn't leave in the morning without talking to her first.

"You swear?" she asked.

"I won't let 'im leave," Jesse said. "I swear."

"Don't worry," Clint said. "We'll meet you at the café down the street at eight."

"I'll be there," she said. "You won't be sorry."

She turned and walked off, a happy spring in her step.

"How old you think she is?" Jesse asked.

"Hard to tell," Clint said.

"Why?"

"It's the skins," Clint said, "and the dirt." He looked closely at Jesse. "Works the same way on you. Nobody knows how old you are."

"And nobody's gonna know," Jesse said. "Ain't nobody's business. Come on, let's eat."

Cole went out once his men were in their rooms. He wanted to know where Jesse Trapp and his friend were staying. He was on the street when he saw Trapp and the other man walking down the street. He stayed across from them, moving along slowly until they went into a café.

He crossed the street, thought about it, then decided to go on in and have something to eat, too. He doubted Trapp would recognize him from the saloon in Little

Town. He was pretty certain the older man had never looked at him.

He went inside.

Clint saw the man enter. He and Jesse had just ordered bowls of stew.

"Don't be obvious about it," he said, "but take a look at the man who just came in."

Jesse barely moved his head and took a look as the man was seated at a table. There were several other tables also occupied.

"Know him?" Clint asked.

"Never seen him."

"He could have been in the saloon in Little Town when you were telling your stories."

"I was drinkin' and tellin' tales," Jesse said. "He coulda been standin' next to me. I still don't know 'im."

Clint didn't look at the man, anymore.

"Ya wanna go and talk to 'im?" Jesse asked. "See if he's followin' us?"

"No," Clint said, "he'll just say no. Forget it. If he's following us we'll catch him in the act sooner or later."

The stew came and they dug in, soaking up the gravy with chunks of crusty bread.

Cole West ordered a steak, rare with everything. When it came he tucked in to his dinner, ignoring Trapp and the other man. He'd find out who that was later, after he finished eating.

He'd left his men in their rooms. They were hungry, but he told them to stay put and he'd bring them something. He'd talk to the waiter about it when he paid his check.

He knew Trapp and his friend were in the same hotel he was in, which meant they probably also had rooms in the same hotel as Shoemaker and Truett. He'd have to go and check the register and finally find out who the other man was.

He ate slowly to make sure that Trapp and his partner finished and left before he did.

Clint and Jesse didn't look at the man as they left. Outside, though, they stopped.

"Let's check the hotel registers," Clint said, "find out who's checked in tonight."

"You think you're gonna recognize the name when you see it?"

"Maybe not," Clint said, "but we can find out how many people checked in."

"And figure they're all here for us?"

"It would be safer to assume that, yes," Clint said. "It's a little too coincidental to have strangers come into town the same time as us."

"We're strangers," Jesse said.

"I know. Come on."

"Why don't we split up?"

"Whether we're dealing with two-legged vermin, or four-, we better start watching each other's back."

"Agreed."

"Also," Clint said, "you can't read."

"Oh, yeah," Jesse Trapp said with a laugh. "I forgot about that."

TWENTY-ONE

Cole watched the two men from the window. He saw them go into one of the hotels, the one he wasn't staying in. Apparently they had the same idea: They were all going to identify each other by name. It would be interesting to see what happened after that.

He went back to his meal.

Evangeline went back to her room, which was behind the livery stable. All she had was a small room with a pallet and a straw-filled mattress. The owner of the livery let her stay there rent-free as long as she did some work for him. There was also a small potbellied stove that kept her warm.

She sat on her bed and cleaned her weapons, made sure they were in proper working order. After all, she was going to be riding with the Gunsmith. That was something she never anticipated. The wolfer Jesse Trapp, yes. But not Clint Adams.

This was going to be an experience she'd remember for a long time.

Clint and Jesse collected the names of the strangers who had checked into the hotels that day. They found out from each clerk that the men named Shoemaker and Truett checked in together, and the men named West and Willis had also checked in together.

They then went back to their hotel after Jesse bought a bottle of whiskey from the saloon. They settled down in Jesse's room. Clint didn't want to do it in his room, because he was afraid the smell of Jesse's skins would keep him awake.

"You know any of these four names?" he asked Jesse.

Jesse rubbed his jaw, took a swig of whiskey from the bottle. He offered it to Clint, who declined.

"Shoemaker?" Clint asked.

"No. Never met anybody named Shoemaker."

"Truett?"

"That name, either."

"Willis?"

"I knew a Willis once, but he's dead."

"How'd he die?"

"Old age."

"Think this could be a son? A grandson?"

"Maybe."

"Why would he be after you?"

"Don't know," Jesse said. "I never did nothin' bad to Eddie Willis."

"Okay, how about West?"

"I knowed a few people named West," Jesse said.

"So have I," Clint said. "You cross any of them?"

"Not that I know," Jesse said.

"Okay," Clint said. "So, Willis and West. Maybe we ought to get a look at those two."

"How do we do that?" Jesse asked. "Knock on their door?"

"Maybe we can just catch a look at them tomorrow in the daylight, before we leave."

"Clint, I came here to hunt for a wolf," Jesse said. "If these men are after me, they should just come ahead and get it over with. I'll get rid of them, and then I'll get rid of the wolf."

"Okay, Jesse," Clint said. "I'm going to go and turn in."

"I'll knock on your door in the mornin'. We'll go eat with that girl."

"Are you really going to want her along with us?" Clint asked.

"I like her skins," Jesse said, "but it ain't gonna matter if she can't shoot or hunt."

"So we'll talk to her and find out," Clint said. "You might want to take it easy on that bottle, Jesse."

"This bottle's gonna keep me warm, Clint," Jesse said. "Don't you worry. I'll be okay come mornin'."

"Okay, Jesse. Goodnight."

Clint left Jesse's room and appreciated the fresh stale air in his own room.

Cole West looked at the name on the register: Clint Adams. Damn, he thought, Jesse Trapp's got the Gunsmith helping him.

He wondered how he was going to share this piece of
news to his three partners. They had come here to help
him kill Jesse Trapp, and now they were going to find
themselves facing the Gunsmith. That might end up
being a little more than they bargained for.

Four to two; that was still pretty good odds, wasn't
it?

TWENTY-TWO

Cole went down to the lobby to talk to the desk clerk.

"You need somethin'?" the clerk asked.

"Yeah, I do," Cole said, "a woman. Is there a whorehouse around here?"

"There's whores," the man said. "There ain't no whorehouse."

"So can you get me a whore to come to my room?" Cole asked.

"Yeah, I can get you a whore."

Something occurred to him at that moment.

"Can you get me four whores?"

"Four?"

"That's right. Two to this hotel, two to the hotel down the street."

"Um, I'd have to arrange it with the desk clerk at the other hotel."

"That's okay."

"We'd, uh, both have to get paid."

"I'll pay the girls."

"Well, yeah, you pay the girls," the clerk said, "but we get paid, too."

"Is that right?"

Cole stared at the man.

"I mean, uh, we don't have to be paid much," the man said uncomfortably.

"Are these decent girls?"

"Decent?" The man grinned. "If they was decent they wouldn't be whores."

"I mean are they good-lookin'," Cole said. "Clean."

"They ain't got no diseases, if that's what you mean," the clerk said. "And they look good enough. I mean . . . what age are you interested in?"

"Do you have that much of a choice?"

"Well . . . no. We actually do have . . . well, four in town."

"All right," Cole said. "Get them all here, and then I'll tell them where to go."

"And payment?"

"We'll talk about payment after I see the women."

"Okay."

"How long will it take to get them here?"

"About twenty minutes, I guess. One of them lives . . . just outside of town."

"All right," Cole said. "Have them come to my room when they get here."

"Okay, Mr. Cole."

"What's your name?"

"Chester."

"Chester," Cole said, "don't tell them anything. I'll talk to them."

"Yessir. Okay."

Clint looked out the window of his room at the darkened, snow-covered streets. He suspected it was not always as dark at that time of the day. It was the storm clouds that were dropping the snow on the town.

Oddly, he saw four figures moving down the street. By craning his neck, he was able to see that they were going to the other hotel.

He also saw that they were all women.

Cole answered the knock on his door, saw the four women in the hall.

"Chester sent us up," one said. She seemed to be the oldest, probably over forty.

"Come in," Cole said.

They entered. All were bundled up with coats or blankets. They looked surprised when they saw he was the only man in the room.

"Four girls all for you?" one of the others asked. She seemed to be the youngest, about twenty-two or twenty-three.

"Oh, there are four men," he said, "but we're in different rooms, and different hotels."

"Well then," the older one said, "who goes where?"

"Well, first I have to see you without your coats."

"Coats, girls," the older one said.

"What's your name?" Cole asked her.

"Diane."

The girls began to remove their layers. Two of them were wearing simple cotton dresses; two had on cotton shirts and denim pants.

Diane was wearing pants, which hugged her curves. She was a solidly built, dark-haired woman. He would send her to Shoemaker.

The young one was blonde, and slender. Her dress showed that she had hardly any breasts or hips. Her name was Mary. He was going to send her to Truett.

The third one had red hair, was in her early thirties. She was tall and gracefully built, with freckles across her nose. He wanted to see if she had freckles elsewhere, so he decided to keep her for himself. She was called Kelsey.

That left the fourth girl for Willis. She was in her late twenties, plain looking, slender but with enormous breasts that strained the seams of her dress. Willis would like that. Her name was Helen. He saw the imprint of a wedding ring on her hand. She was probably married and making some extra money for her family. He wondered how many of the others were also married.

"Okay," he said, pointing to Kelsey, "you'll stay here with me."

"Okay," she said with a shrug.

"Helen, come with me."

"All right."

He went out into the hall, pulling her by the hand. He knocked when they reached Willis's door.

Willis answered the door and said, "What?"

"This one's yours," Cole said, pushing Helen toward him. She bumped into him and bounced off.

"Jesus," Willis said, "look at the teats on her!"

"Treat her right."

"She ain't that pretty, though."

"Send her away, then."

"Hell no," Willis said, pulling Helen into the room. "I wanna see what's under that dress."

Cole walked to his own room. Willis stuck his head into the hall.

"Am I payin' her?"

"I'm takin' care of it!" Cole yelled back.

Back in his room, he said to Diane and Mary, "You'll go over to the other hotel, room five. There's two fellas there named Shoemaker and Truett. Diane, tell Shoemaker you're his."

"And I guess that makes Mary Truett's," Diane said. "See how smart I am?"

"You better put your coats back on."

As they did Diane asked, "What about our money?"

"Chester said I had to pay him."

"He ain't our pimp," she said. "You pay me and I pay the girls. If you wanna pay Chester somethin', that's between you and him."

"Okay."

"You wanna know our price?"

He took a bunch of money from his pocket and pushed it into her hands.

"That enough?"

Diane looked at the money and said, "For a week."

"Just one night, darlin'," he told her. "Just one night."

"Come on, Mary."

Diane and Mary walked out, leaving Kelsey with Cole.

"Okay," he said. "show me all your freckles."

"All of 'em?" she asked.

"Yep."

"That's gonna take a while."

"We got all night."

She started to undress.

TWENTY-THREE

Clint watched two of the women come out of the other hotel and walk across the street to his. Apparently one of the strangers was buying women for the other three. Or for all four of them. He wondered how many whores were plying their trade in Wolf Creek? Maybe Jesse would want one to go with his bottle of whiskey.

He walked to his bed, sat down, and pulled off his boots. His gun was hanging on the bedpost. He took it from its holster and set about to cleaning it, then did the same with his rifle.

He heard the women walk past his door and move on down the hall. He listened, heard a door open and close.

When he was done with his guns he sat on the bed and opened a book: Robert Louis Stevenson's *Treasure Island*. He'd been meaning to start it for a long time. Now was as good a time as any.

He read two chapters, then doused the light and got underneath the blanket.

* * *

A knock at Clint's door woke him a short time later. He grabbed his gun and took it with him. Opened the door and saw Jesse standing there. Actually, he was weaving. He peered owlishly at Clint, looking unhappy.

"What's wrong?" Clint asked.

"Tried to get me a whore for the night," Jesse said. "You know what the desk clerk tol' me? Ain't no whore-house, and they're only four whores in the whole town, and they's busy tonight."

"Yeah," Clint said. "I saw them while I was looking out the window. Two of them are in the hotel across the street, and two are over here."

"Here?" Jesse looked up and down the hall. "Where?"

"I don't know," Clint said. "In one of the rooms, with the other strangers."

"Well, gawdamn . . ."

Clint wondered if Jesse had finished that entire bottle of whiskey.

"Jesse . . . why don't you go back to your room and go to sleep?"

"Ain't sleepy."

"You finish that bottle of whiskey?"

"Sure did."

Now Clint was amazed that the man was even walking, let alone looking for a woman.

"Come on," Clint said. "I'll take you back to your room."

As they walked, Jesse asked, "You think them fellers is gonna keep them whores all night?"

"It's kind of cold tonight," Clint said. "I'd guess they are."

"Well, gawdamn."

Clint found Jesse's door open, pushed his friend into the room, and closed the door behind them. He walked him to the bed and deposited the man on it.

"Don't like these hotel rooms," Jesse muttered. "Rather be sleepin' outside."

For someone who'd rather be sleeping outside, he fell right to sleep and started snoring.

Clint almost pulled Jesse's boots off, but considering the smell of the skins he didn't want to deal with the smell of his socks. Instead he just tossed a blanket over him and left the room.

He went back to his room, passing another from where he thought he heard familiar sounds—bedsprings, and women. He made a mental note of the room number.

TWENTY-FOUR

Dave Willis rolled over in bed the next morning and saw the woman lying next to him. She was on her back, which made her big breasts flatten out and lean to either side of her rib cage. Asleep, her face was as plain as could be, with thin lips and sunken cheeks. Her body was slender, her legs long and skinny, but those breasts . . . For a man who liked women with big chests, he could forgive her anything. He leaned over, grabbed one breast in his hand and hefted it, then brought it to his mouth so he could bite her nipple.

"Ow! What the—" She jerked awake, saw him grinning down at her, and remembered where she was and what she was doing. She was trying to make some money to feed her three kids, because her husband was out of work. That meant she had to be nice to this man, who was quite possibly the worst she'd ever been with. All he wanted to do was bite her tits.

And she had to be nice about it.

"Hey," she said, smiling at him, holding her right breast in her hands, "don't forget the other one . . ."

Cole woke with a warm hip next to him, turned his head. Kelsey was asleep with her face toward him, and he looked again at the freckles on her nose. Once she'd undressed he'd been able to see just how many freckles she had—on the slopes of her breasts, on her shoulders, even a few around her rusty-colored nipples. Asleep, she was extraordinarily pretty. It had been a pleasant night, and he knew he'd made the right choice keeping her for himself.

She opened her eyes, as if she knew she was being stared at.

"Mornin'," she said, stretching and making her small breasts go taut.

Kelsey was the only whore in town who didn't have a man of her own. She didn't think it would be fair to a man, considering what she did for money. The other women all had husbands who weren't bringing money in, even young Mary. Her husband was twenty and useless.

She rolled over, put her hand on Cole's chest, then moved it down over his belly until she was grasping him firmly.

"Oh, somebody is very awake," she said, sliding a leg over him.

Across the street, Diane and Mary slipped from the hotel room as their men slept, snoring loudly. They hadn't particularly enjoyed doing their jobs in beds next to each other, but both men had just rolled over and fallen asleep after a few minutes.

They left the hotel and went back home to their families. Diane would pay the other women later in the day.

Cole West had Kelsey down on all fours, fucking her from behind while she grunted and groaned. He ran his hands over her back. The combined heat from their rutting bodies had raised the temperature in the room to the point where they were both sweating.

Kelsey braced her hands on the mattress and drove her butt back into Cole as he thrusted forward. She had to admit she was enjoying her job this night, as opposed to the way things usually went.

"Yeah, ooh yeah, that's it," she exhorted him. "More . . . harder . . . faster . . . ohh baby . . ."

Cole tried his best to give her what she wanted while also getting what he wanted. He smacked her ass until it glowed red, and still she implored him to go on . . .

Clint woke early the next morning. The room was cold, the water from the pitcher even colder as he washed his face and torso. Shivering, he dried himself and walked to the window. The snow had stopped, but a coat of it covered the ground. There were no people out yet, and maybe there wouldn't be, since they were all afraid of the wolf.

He got dressed and had just strapped on his gun when there was a knock at the door.

He was surprised to see Jesse Trapp standing there, dressed and fresh-looking.

"You ready?" Jesse asked.

"Jesus," Clint said, "I thought I'd have to come to your room and drag you out of bed."

"Take more than a little ol' bottle of whiskey to put me under," Trapp said.

"I guess so."

"Come on," Jesse said, "I'm hungry."

They walked down to the lobby, where they saw two women talking with the desk clerk. The pair turned as Clint and Jesse came down; the younger of the two averted her eyes, looking almost guilty. Clint assumed these were two part-time whores.

He and Jesse left the hotel.

TWENTY-FIVE

Cole could have stayed in bed with Kelsey all day, she was that good. But that wasn't what he had come to Wolf Creek to do.

He shooed her out of his room, walked down the hall to Dave Willis's room, and knocked.

"What?" Willis shouted from inside.

"Come on, time to get up!"

"Go away."

Cole pounded on the door until Willis finally opened it. The man was naked, with a raging erection. Behind him, on the bed, Cole saw the big-breasted whore on her knees, watching the two of them. She did nothing to try and hide those big tits, which were firmer and did not hang down as far as Cole had thought they would. Her plain face looked puzzled, but he had to admit she had nice skin and pretty pink nipples.

"We gotta go," Cole said. "Send her home."

"But I ain't done!" Willis said.

Cole looked down at Willis's dick, which was softening.

"Yeah, you are. Come on, get dressed and meet me in the lobby."

"Yeah, yeah, okay," Willis said and slammed the door.

Cole waited in the lobby. While he was waiting, he looked out the door and saw Jesse Trapp and Clint Adams come out of the other hotel and walk to the café.

Eventually Willis came down with the girl and slapped her on the rump as she went out the front door.

"Did you see the tits on that one?" Willis asked. "Gawd!"

"Forget about that now," Cole said. "We got to go and get Shoe and Truett. Trapp and his man are in the café."

"How are we gonna eat if they're there?" Willis complained.

"I don't know," Cole said. "Maybe there's someplace else."

"I'll ask the clerk."

"We'll ask the one across the street," Cole said. "Come on."

When Shoe and Truett opened their door Cole looked in and saw that the whores were gone. The room was warm from naked bodies, and smelled stale.

"I'm starvin'," Shoemaker complained.

"Just wait," Cole said. "We got to come in. I got somethin' to tell you all."

"What's goin' on?" Truett asked as Cole and Willis entered.

"He's got somethin' ta tell us," Shoemaker said. "Don't sound like good news."

"Aw, damn," Truett said. "I don't like bad news."

"Nobody does. Shut the door," he told Willis.

The door slammed. Willis was still miffed at having to send his whore home.

"What's goin' on, Cole?" he asked.

"I found out who the other man with Trapp is."

"That's the bad news?" Shoe asked.

"Dependin' on how you look at it," Cole said.

"Who is it?" Truett asked.

Cole hesitated then said, "It's Clint Adams."

The three men remained silent, and then Willis said, "You mean . . . the Gunsmith?"

"Yeah," Cole said, "That's what I mean."

TWENTY-SIX

When Clint and Jesse got to the café, Evangeline was standing outside.

"Why didn't you go inside and get a table?" Clint asked.

"They wouldn't let me in," she said.

"Why not?"

"They don't think I can pay."

"Hell, kid," Jesse said, "if they'll let me in, they'll let you in. Come on."

The three of them went inside; Clint asked for a table for three people.

Both Jesse and Evangeline drew stares as they walked past people to get to a table.

Clint ordered a pot of coffee. He and Jesse ordered steak and eggs.

Evangeline hesitated.

"What's wrong?" Clint asked.

"Can I have anything I want?"

"Of course you can," Clint said.

She ordered steak and eggs, biscuits and gravy, and flapjacks.

"Are you sure that's everything?" Clint asked.

"That's all," she said. "I know we won't be eatin' much while we're hunting."

"How do you know that?"

"We're gonna be huntin' a wolf," she said. "We ain't gonna wanna build a fire and start cookin' somethin' that'll attract it."

"Why not?" Jesse asked. "We wanna find him, don't we?"

"Yeah," she said, "but not in our camp. We wanna find him on our terms."

Jesse looked at Clint, who just shrugged.

"Let me see your rifle," Clint asked.

"Sure."

She handed over her Winchester. Clint checked it, found it in perfect working order, and recently cleaned. He handed it back.

"Got anything else?" he asked.

From inside her skins she produced a handgun, a worn but well-cared-for Colt. He looked it over, then handed that back, as well.

"You care for your weapons well."

"If my guns fail me on a hunt, I'm dead," she said.

"That's true," Jesse said.

The waiter came with their breakfasts, and filled Evangeline's side of the table with food. The two men watched in awe as she plowed through it.

"After we eat," Jesse said to Clint, "we'll pack the mule, mount up, and get movin'."

"We've got to wait for Thompson," Clint said, but just then the ranch hand walked in and approached their table.

"Sorry I'm late," he said. "I got time to eat?"

"Sure," Jesse said. "Order somethin', if you can find some room on the table."

"All that food hers?" he asked, sitting down.

"Yeah," Evangeline said. "Don't touch."

"I won't," he said, "but those flapjacks look good." The waiter came over and he ordered a stack.

"I wanna see the two places where men were killed," Jesse said to Thompson.

"That ain't a problem, but with this fresh snow you ain't gonna be able to find nothin'."

"Don't worry about it," Jesse said. "I just wanna have a look."

Thompson looked at Clint. "I'm curious. Why are you here, Mr. Adams?"

"Jesse asked me along," Clint said. "That was all the reason I needed. And we might as well all be on a first-name basis, Lee."

"Me, too?" Evangeline asked.

"Yes," Clint said, "you, too. Call me Clint."

"You can call me Evie," she said.

The waiter came over with a stack of flapjacks, maple syrup, and butter.

"Are your guns in working order?" Clint asked Thompson.

Thompson nodded. "I cleaned 'em last night."

"Good. Are you a good shot?"

"I can usually hit what I aim at."

"Me, too," Evangeline said.

"Maybe," Clint said, "when we get out of town I can see the two of you shoot."

"Evangeline is right," Thompson said. "I've seen her shoot. She's good."

"Thanks, Lee," she said, "but why wouldn't your boss let me come along when you fellas went out?"

"I told him you could shoot, Evie," the man said. "He just didn't want no women along. Only his own men."

"I guess I could understand that," Jesse said.

"You're lettin' me come along," she pointed out.

"Yeah, but I got my man along—Clint. We'll watch each other's back."

"Well, Evie," Lee Thompson said, "I guess we'll just have to watch each other's backs, too."

"Don't worry," Clint said. "We'll be watching each other. All four of us."

TWENTY-SEVEN

"We gotta go up against the Gunsmith?" Shoemaker asked.

Cole nodded.

"You know, Cole," Truett said, "we all came up here as a favor to you. We all liked your brothers, and want to help you get your revenge, but even Link and Harve ain't worth dyin' over."

"Look," Cole said, "Adams is out of his element here. Plus he can't be as good as his rep says. He just can't. I think since we still got them outnumbered four to two, we're okay."

"Even if his rep is only half true, I ain't happy about goin' up agin him," Shoemaker said.

"We kill him and Trapp, we avenge my brothers, and we make names for ourselves. You know how much money you can make if you're known as one of the men who killed Clint Adams?"

"Well," Willis said, "there is that."

"So what do we do now?" Shoemaker said.

"Adams and Trapp are in the café," Cole said. "We gotta keep an eye on them and see what they're gonna do today."

"So we can't eat?" Shoemaker asked.

"Shoe, you find out from the desk clerk where else we could eat," Cole said. "The rest of us will watch the café. If you find someplace else to eat, you all can go and I'll keep an eye on them."

"Sounds okay to me," Truett said.

"And if they decide to leave town and start huntin' today?" Willis asked.

"Then so will we," Cole said.

It didn't work the way they planned.

There was a smaller café around the corner. Cole let the other three go, hid in a doorway across the street, and watched the first café. When Adams and Trapp came out they had two others with them, a man and a girl. Cole didn't know who they were, but they all started walking to the livery together.

He ran to get his men.

Lee Thompson's horse was saddled and waiting outside when they came out. He walked with them to the livery and waited while they packed the mule and saddled their horses. None of the food they had been carrying had gone bad, not with how cold it was in the livery.

Once they had all their animals ready they walked

them outside, and mounted up. Evangeline had a six-year-old mare that looked fit enough for what they were going to be doing. Clint didn't anticipate that any of these other mounts would have to keep up with Eclipse on the dead run.

"Where's the first place?" Jesse asked Thompson.

"A ranch just outside of town," Thompson said. "Should take us about twenty minutes to get there."

"Okay," Clint said. "Lead the way."

Thompson took the lead and they walked out of Wolf Creek single file. Once they got outside of town, Evangeline rode up alongside of Clint.

"So you're really the Gunsmith?" she asked.

"I really am."

"You kill as many men as they say you have?"

"No."

"Then why do they say it?"

"People like to talk," he said.

"So it's all lies, what they say about you?"

"Not all," he said, "but a lot."

"Gee . . ."

"How old are you, Evie?"

"I'm twenty."

"Have you got folks around here?"

"I did," she said, "but they died a few years ago. Been on my own since then."

"Seems like you take good care of yourself."

"I try," she said. "I can make my own money when somebody'll hire me to hunt."

"Can you do anything else?" he asked.

"Like what?"

"Waitress, or work in a store."

"God, no!" she said. "I'd rather be dead. I can ride, I can hunt, and I can shoot. That's all I wanna do."

"Well, okay," he said. "Then that's all we'll have to do until we find that wolf."

"Well," she said, "I can cook when I'm on the trail."

"I make the best trail coffee," he said.

"Bet mine's better," she said with a grin.

"Well," he said, "we'll see about that."

Cole, Willis, Shoemaker, and Truett watched the four riders walk their horses out of the livery. Shoemaker and Truett were still holding some biscuits, finishing their breakfast on the run.

"Now, who are they?" Willis complained.

"They're probably just guides," Cole said. "Trapp and Adams have to be shown to where the wolf had its kills."

"And what do we do?" Truett asked.

"We trail them."

"Again?" Shoemaker asked.

"We just need to bide our time a little more," Cole said.

"The four of us followin' the four of them?" Willis asked. "You think they ain't gonna notice?"

"We still got the snow to work with," Cole said. "We don't have to follow them close, just track 'em."

"They're outfitted," Shoemaker said. "We got no supplies."

He was right.

"Okay," Cole said, "me and Willis will track 'em.

You and Truett pick up some supplies, just whatever you can carry. Then you catch up to us."

"I don't like this," Shoemaker said.

"Shoe, it's all gonna work out," Cole said. "I guarantee you."

TWENTY-EIGHT

Thompson led them to a small ranch. There was a two-room house, a barn, and a corral.

"Lou Jacks lived here," he said, "until that damn wolf killed him."

"Right here?" Jesse asked. "Right on his property?"

"The wolf was in the corral, killin' a horse when Lou heard him. He come runnin' out with his rifle, but he never got off a shot."

"Did you see 'im?" Jesse asked.

"I saw 'im."

"Show me where he was."

Thompson led them to the corral. "He was right in there, lying on his back with his throat ripped out."

"Where was his rifle?" Clint asked.

"Over there."

"How far from the body?" Clint asked.

"'Bout ten feet."

Clint got in the corral and walked over to where the body had been lying.

"And the horse? Did the wolf kill it?"

"Oh yeah," Thompson said. "Got its throat, too. It was lyin' right there."

"So he came out here with his rifle," Clint said. "Why'd he get in the corral? Why not shoot the wolf from outside?"

"Dunno," Jesse said, "but he did."

"He came into the corral, probably got hit here," Clint said. "His rifle went flying. He never had a chance."

"The wolf musta hit him so fast," Evie said.

"Wolves are fast, all right," Jesse said.

They all stood there a few moments, then Clint got out of the corral.

"Okay," Jesse said, "where did the sheriff get it?"

"I'll show you," Thompson said.

They mounted up again.

"Where is it?" Jesse asked as they started off.

"The other side of town."

"Not near here?"

"No."

"That far away? You sure it was the same wolf?"

"Well, no," Thompson said, "we ain't dead sure it was the same wolf."

"How do we know it was a white wolf that killed both men?" Jesse asked.

"Well, somebody saw a white wolf around Lou's place," Thompson said.

"What about where the sheriff was killed?" Jesse asked.

"Dunno."

"What was the sheriff doin' when he got killed?" Jesse asked.

"He was just ridin'," Thompson said. "Comin' back to town from one of the ranches."

"He wasn't huntin' the wolf?" Jesse asked.

"Nope. Sheriff weren't no hunter. He also wasn't much of a sheriff."

"What's the deputy like?" Clint asked. "We haven't talked to him yet."

"He's just a kid," Thompson said. "They're gonna have to appoint a sheriff real soon."

"How far is this place?" Jesse asked.

"Other side of town, I said," Thompson replied. "If we go around town and not through it'll take about an hour."

"Still," Jesse said, "let's go around. I wanna get the lay of the land."

"Around it is," Clint said. "Lead the way, Lee."

TWENTY-NINE

"What are they doin'?" Willis complained. He hated the cold.

"I heard in town," Cole said. "Two men were killed by a wolf. One of them musta lived here."

"And the other one?"

"I guess that's where they're goin' now."

"Great," Willis said. "Why don't we just shoot them now and be done with it?"

"Because if the other two are just scouts, they'll be gone soon."

"Then we can take the other two."

Cole looked at Willis.

"When I say so."

Willis shook his head, but kept quiet. He didn't really understand why Cole was going through all this trouble, and Jesse Trapp wasn't even the man who'd actually killed his brothers. But he'd go along because he said he would.

And because he was afraid of Cole West.

*   *   *

"Here," Thompson said. He looked around, then nodded. "Yeah, here."

"You sure?" Jesse asked.

"I think so."

"It don't look right," Jesse said.

"Why not?" Evie asked.

"We're on the road," Jesse said. "What's a wolf doin' attackin' a man on the road?"

"Or on his own property, for that matter," Clint added.

"Yeah, right," Jesse said. "This wolf don't seem to be like no other wolf."

"Well," Evie said, "it's white," as if that explained it all.

They all looked at her.

"Well, ain't white wolves different?" she asked.

"Yeah," Jesse said, "they're different . . . but this one is too different. I don't like it." He looked at Lee Thompson. "Where was the sheriff's horse? Did the wolf get away?"

"Yeah, it came back to town without him, which is why folks went lookin' for him."

"And where'd they find him?"

"Way I heard it, they found him in the road," Thompson said.

"You didn't see 'im?"

"No, I didn't see the sheriff," Thompson said, "but I heard they found him in the road with his throat tore out."

Jesse got down and walked the ground, staring intently. Clint couldn't see anything, but he knew that didn't mean a thing. He was good at reading signs, but he wasn't in Jesse Trapp's class.

"It hasn't been back since the snow fell," he announced, mounting up again.

"So what do we do?" Evie asked.

Jesse looked at Clint.

"I don't like that it killed two men so far apart," he said. "I'm thinkin' we might have more than one wolf— which really makes more sense. They usually do hunt in packs."

"Jesus, if there's more than one, the town is gonna panic—" Thompson started.

"We don't say anything about this," Clint said. "It's only a theory. There's no use panicking the town. Understood?"

"Sure," Thompson said.

"I understand," Evie said.

"Good."

"No point in us goin' back to town," Jesse said. "We'll start from here."

"Lee," Clint said, "you can go back. Tell your boss what's going on, but don't talk to anyone else."

"I won't. What about her?"

"Evie's stayin' with us," Jesse said. "We can use somebody who knows the area."

Thompson shrugged as if he didn't care. "When will you be back?" he asked. "My boss is gonna wanna know."

"We won't be back in," Jesse said, "until we done what we came to do."

Thompson nodded again, said, "Good luck," then turned his horse and rode back toward town.

"We got enough supplies for that?" Evie asked Jesse.

It was Clint who answered her. "We do if you don't eat again like you did this morning," he said.

"Don't worry 'bout me," she said. "I can make do on coffee and jerky."

"We'll do a little better than that," Jesse said, "but not much."

"They're riding across," Cole said, "making it easier to track."

Willis seemed uninterested.

"And look."

"What?" Willis asked.

"There's only three now."

"So one of them went back to town," Willis said. "Now it's four to three."

"Unless the girl is still with them, acting as a guide," Cole said. "Then it's four to two."

"Unless she's Annie Oakley," Willis said.

"What are the chances of that?" Cole said.

Willis remained silent.

"Hold up," Cole said, reining in.

"What?" Willis asked.

"Well, look." He pointed down.

Willis looked.

"I don't see—"

"The wolf track," Cole said.

"Oh." Willis said. "So they found it and are trackin' it?"

"No, look at it," Cole said. "It's behind them. The wolf is trackin' them!"

THIRTY

"Maybe we should've kept Mr. Thompson," Jesse said sometime later.

"Why's that?" Clint asked.

"Then we could have had two of us look around here, and two look around at that ranch, where the first man got killed."

"This is where the second kill took place," Evie said. "Ain't that better? To start here, I mean?"

"Yeah," Jesse said, "if there's only one wolf."

"I hope there's only one," Clint said.

They rode three abreast, with Evie in between them.

"I don't," Jesse said.

"Why?" Evie asked.

"Because they usually hunt in packs," Jesse said. "A lone wolf . . . well, that's different."

"But a white—"

"I know, I know," Jesse said, "a white's different, anyway. But got to remember, a white is still a gray."

"So?" she asked.

"It should still be with a pack. Unless . . ."

"Unless what?" Clint asked.

"Unless its pack is gone, or dead. Or it could have a mate and some pups in the area. Maybe it's protectin' them."

"They'd be in a cave somewhere, right?" Clint asked.

"Probably."

"Where are there some caves around here, Evie?" Clint asked.

"North of here," she said, pointing.

"Take us there," Jesse said. "Likely be a cave it'd be takin' refuge in, anyway."

"Okay," she said, "this way."

"Up there," she said, sometime later, pointing.

"Leave the horses here," Jesse said. "Let's go and look for some tracks."

They all dismounted. Jesse and Evie tied their horses loosely, Clint not at all. If there was a wolf around, he wanted Eclipse to be able to run—or fight.

They walked up the slope toward the caves.

"Stop!" Jesse said.

They did.

"Look."

Clint and Evie both saw what he was pointing at: wolf tracks in the fresh snow.

"This is too easy," Jesse said.

"Nobody else came to look in the caves," Evie told him. "Ever."

Jesse looked at Clint.

"Not everybody knows about wolves and caves," Clint said.

"Maybe not . . ."

"I notice somethin' else," Evie said.

"Oh yeah?" Jesse asked. "What's that, little lady?"

"These tracks come out," she said, "but there are none goin' back in."

"That's real good."

"So it came out after last night's snow," Clint said, "and hasn't been back in, yet."

"It's out there," Jesse said, "somewhere."

At that moment they heard shots.

"What the—" Evie said.

"Where's that comin' from?" Jesse asked.

"Not from near here," Clint said.

"How can you tell?" Evie asked.

"We're not hearing shots," Clint said. "We're hearing the echo of shots."

When they heard the shots, the men turned in their saddles to look behind them.

"Damn," Willis said. "What the hell?"

"That ain't far behind us," Cole said. "Come on."

They turned their horses and rode back the way they had come.

Cole and Willis rode into a clearing and stopped short.

"Jesus Christ," Willis said.

The snow in the entire clearing was red with blood. And lying there with their throats torn out were Shoemaker and Truett.

"A wolf did this?" Willis asked.

Cole looked around for their horses, but the animals must have run off in panic, maybe with the wolf in pursuit.

"We gotta find their horses," Cole said. "We're gonna need those supplies."

"Supplies?" Willis asked. "They're dead, Cole."

"I can see that, Dave."

"We gotta get out of here."

"I ain't leavin' until Trapp is dead," Cole said. "And if you try to leave, Dave, I'll kill you. So you and me are gonna go and look for those horses."

"What about them?" Willis asked. "Don't we gotta bury them?"

"No," Cole said. "I ain't gonna be caught on the ground by that wolf. Now let's go."

Willis thought Cole had a point. Being on the ground wasn't a good idea. He wondered if Shoe and Truett had been on the ground, or if the wolf had somehow taken them out of their saddles.

Just the thought of that was scary.

They listened, but there were no more shots—or echoes of shots.

"Could be anything," Clint said.

"Hunters," Evie said.

"I said nobody was to come out lookin' for that wolf while we was out here," Jesse said.

"Maybe," Clint said, "they'll panic and end up killing each other."

"I hope so," Jesse said. "Better than havin' some amateur kill us."

THIRTY-ONE

They walked around in front of the caves for a few minutes, each in a different direction until Jesse called out.

Clint and Evie ran to join him.

"There," he said.

"Wolf tracks, coming out, but not going back in."

"We know that," Clint said.

"No, look closer," Jesse said.

They did.

Clint shook his head. "I don't get it."

"I do," Evie said.

Both men looked at her.

"That's a second wolf," she said. "The tracks are slightly different."

"Good," Jesse said, impressed.

"They're a little smaller," she added.

"True," Jesse said.

"A female?" Clint asked.

"Could be two males," Jesse said, "one full-grown, one not."

"How do we tell?" Clint asked.

"That part's easy," Jesse said. "We find 'em."

"What's the hard part?"

"Killin' them before they kill us."

"I'm gonna go into the cave," Jesse said, taking his Big Fifty from his saddle.

"Why?" Evie said. "They're out here."

"There might be cubs inside."

"And if there is?" she asked.

"I'll kill 'em."

"What?"

"We can't just wait for them to grow up and then kill 'em," he said.

"But . . . they're babies."

"They're wolves," he said.

"Clint?"

"Don't look at me," Clint said. "He's the hunter. What he says goes."

"Can I go in with you?" she asked Jesse.

"What for?"

"If there are cubs, I wanna see 'em."

"Why? That'll just make it worse for you when I kill 'em," he said. "Or do you think if you go with me you can keep me from killin' them?"

"I—well, no—"

"Because you won't," Jesse said. "This is my job. And if you're a hunter, it's yours, too."

"Well—"

"In fact, you know what? You can come with me. And if we find the cubs, you can kill 'em."

"No," she said, "I don't think—I better stay out here with Clint and watch his back. He'll be all exposed out here."

"Yeah, that's true," Jesse said, as if he hadn't thought of that. "Okay, so you stay outside, while I go in."

"Okay."

Jesse approached the slope.

"You want me to go to the mouth of the cave with you?" Clint asked.

"No," Jesse said, "just find a good-size branch and make me a torch."

"Be good if we had some lamp oil."

"On the mule," Jesse said.

Clint found a thick-enough branch and the oil, pulled a shirt out of his own saddlebags, and wrapped it around the branch. Then he doused it with oil and carried it back to Jesse.

"Here," Clint said, "and take these." He gave Jesse a few lucifer matches.

"Thanks. I'll be out pretty quick if there's nothin' in there. If I find cubs you'll hear my pistol, not the Sharps."

"Okay."

"The Big Fifty would make a mess of a wolf pup," he said.

"Jesus," Evie said.

Jesse hefted his torch and his rifle and worked his way up the slope.

"So what do we do now?" Evie asked Clint.

"Let's wait by the horses," Clint said, "just in case."

"In case what?"

"In case a bunch of wolves come pouring out of that cave."

"You think there might be a pack in here?"

"No," he said, "I just want to make sure the horses, and the mule, don't go anywhere. Come on."

THIRTY-TWO

Cole and Willis found one of the horses, and were able to salvage some of the supplies, including the coffee and beef jerky. The pot was already in Cole's saddlebag.

"Now what?" Willis asked.

"We've got to get back on Trapp's trail," Cole said.

"Cole, maybe we should go back."

"No!" Cole said. "I've come this far, I ain't givin' up now."

"We could get help—"

"We don't need help," Cole said.

"But there's wolves out here!"

Cole drew his gun.

"You wanna take a chance with wolves or a bullet from my gun?"

"Okay, okay, take it easy," Willis said. "Put the gun away. I'm with you."

Cole holstered the gun and said, "Then let's get goin'."

"Can we go around that clearing?" Willis asked. "I don't wanna see all that blood again."

"Sure," Cole said, "we'll go around."

Cole and Willis picked up the trail again, even after going around the bloody clearing. They followed it, Cole keeping aware so that they wouldn't accidentally just ride up on Adams and Trapp.

"Is that wolf still followin' them, too?" Willis asked.

"Looks like it."

"Jesus . . ."

"Don't worry about it," Cole said. "They're all in front of us."

"Yeah, sure . . ." Willis said, looking around nervously.

Cole had to admit he was a little nervous, himself. He was ready to deal with Jesse Trapp or the Gunsmith, but some bloodthirsty wolf was another story. The animal must have moved incredibly fast to take both Shoemaker and Truett with only a few shots fired. Maybe they'd wounded it, but he hoped not. He'd heard all the stories about how much more dangerous animals were when they were injured.

Maybe Trapp would do his job and take care of the wolf before they took care of Trapp.

Clint and Evie watched as Jesse went up the slope to the mouth of the cave, paused to light his torch, and then went inside.

"Will he really kill the pups?" she asked.

"Oh, yeah," Clint said. "That's what he does. He kills wolves."

"But pups?"

"They'll grow up to be wolves," Clint reminded her.

Abruptly, Jesse's horse tossed its head and nickered.

"Somebody's out there," she said. "Maybe the wolf?"

"No," he said.

"Why not?"

"Because if there was a wolf out there, *my* horse would be letting me know."

And just at that moment Eclipse made a slight noise.

"But somebody is out there," Clint said. "Probably men."

"From town," she said.

"Or the men who have been following us."

"You had men followin' you up here?"

"Yeah, we think they have a beef with Jesse."

"Why haven't they tried anything?"

"They're probably waiting for the right time."

"And when would that be?"

"When everything is in their favor."

"So they might be watching us right now?" she asked, looking around.

"If they are," Clint said, "it's not a good idea to look around and let them know we know they're there."

She turned her head and looked at him. "Sorry."

"Just keep watching the mouth of the cave," Clint told her.

"Okay."

As she turned her head they heard several shots. The echo was so loud, they must have come from inside the cave.

"Get ready," Clint said, "just in case."

Evie held her rifle tightly. They both watched the cave entrance, waiting for either Jesse or some wolves to come out.

Finally, Jesse Trapp came walking out, threw down the torch so that the snow snuffed it out, and waved.

THIRTY-THREE

"You think he got that wolf?" Willis asked.

"Maybe," Cole said.

"Well, he fired some shots."

"He might've found their den," Cole said, "and shot the pups."

"Jesus," Willis said, "why would he do that?"

"Because pups grow up to be wolves, stupid."

"Yeah, but shootin' pups?"

Cole looked at Willis. "You can shoot a man, but not some wolf pulps?"

"What'd they ever do to anyone?" Willis asked.

"Jesus," Cole said. "You're strange."

They both looked down at the three people again as Trapp approached the other two.

"What're they gonna do now?"

"Don't know," Cole said. "We'll just have to wait and see."

"We can't just . . . take 'em?"

Cole looked down at the group and said, "We'll wait and see."

Jesse came down the slope.

"How many?" Clint asked.

"Three."

"Pups?" Evie asked.

"Yes, pups."

She looked down.

"There ain't another way in or out of that cave that I can see," he said. "They'll have to come back this way to get in."

"They?" she asked.

"There are two, probably mates," he said.

"Both whites?" she asked.

"That I don't know," he said. "We know one is a white because it's been seen. Don't know about the other one, but it's likely a gray."

"What makes you say that?" she asked.

"All the pups were gray."

He took a moment to eject the spent shells from his old Navy Colt handgun and then reload.

"Why don't you get a new gun?" Clint asked.

"This is fine," Jesse said. "Does the job."

Jesse's horse whinnied and shook its head. Jesse didn't look up, but he said, "Somebody's out there."

"Yeah, we figured that out," Clint said. "Don't know if it's man or beast, but I think it's man."

"Or men," Evie said.

Jesse holstered his gun inside his skins again, then looked at Clint.

"What's next?" Evie asked.

"Well we can hunt for the wolves, or we can wait here for them to come back."

"Will they come back with us here?" Clint asked. "And with whoever's out there, watching us?"

"Well," Jesse said, "I believe I have two minds about that."

"And what are they?"

"Either they won't come back because we're all here," Jesse said, "or they will come back here because we're all here."

"What does that mean?" Evie asked.

"It means," Clint said, "that they might come back to hunt us."

"That's right," Jesse said. "That's exactly what I mean."

THIRTY-FOUR

Jesse decided they should move away from the cave and make camp. Then, one at a time, they would watch the mouth of the cave to see if the wolf returned.

"What if it comes after us in camp?" she asked.

"The fire should keep it out," Jesse said.

"And what about our scent?" Clint asked. "Won't that keep it away from the area?"

"Normally, I'd say yes," Jesse said, "but I think he or his mate will come back to check on those pups. To feed them."

"So the draw of the pups will make them ignore the danger?" Evie asked.

"I don't think they'll ignore anythin'," Jesse said. "But I do believe one or both of them will return."

They walked the horses and the mule to a small clearing upwind of the cave, in an attempt to keep their scent to themselves. That done, they tied up the animals and built a fire.

"How we gonna see in the dark?" Evie asked.

"They'll be enough moonlight," Jesse said. "Once your eyes are accustomed to the night, you should be able to see a wolf walking up to that cave."

"And what'll happen when the wolves see that their pups are dead?"

"They'll probably mourn," Jesse said, "and then look for revenge."

"Wolves look for revenge?" she asked.

"Especially the female," Jesse said, "once her pups are dead. You've hunted wolves, Evie. You should know that."

She stared across the fire at him, then at Clint.

"I got a confession to make," she said.

The men both waited.

"I ain't never hunted for no wolf," she said. "Biggest thing I ever shot was a deer."

"Well, what a surprise that is," Jesse said.

"You knowed that?"

"I figured."

"Then why'd you take me along?"

"We needed somebody who knew the area," Jesse said, "and I thought you showed promise."

Clint studied Jesse Trapp. Sometimes he felt the man was smarter than he let on, and that his accent came and went.

"I'm gonna go keep watch on that cave first," Jesse said.

"I'll relieve you in a few hours," Clint said.

"Okay," Jesse said, "but if you hear my Sharps, you come a-runnin'. Both of you."

"Yessir," Clint said.

"What about the men who are after you?" Evie asked.

Jesse looked at Clint, who just shrugged.

"Well, since you know about them," Jesse said, "they won't be able to sneak up on me. I'll hear 'em. If they want me they're gonna have to come out in the open."

"What about me and Clint?"

"Same thing for Clint," he said. "They'll try him out in the open. But you . . ."

"Yeah?"

"You better keep your eyes and ears open," he said, "because they'd probably slit your throat from behind, or kill you in your sleep."

Jesse blended into the brush and was gone.

"Was he kiddin'?" she asked.

"I would say no."

Cole and Willis camped and built a fire. Cole even put on a pot of coffee.

"You don't think they'll smell it?"

"They'll smell their own coffee," Cole said, chewing on a piece of beef jerky.

"What about the wolf?"

"Yeah, it'll smell us and stay away."

"How do you know?" Willis asked. "You ain't a wolf expert."

"I know they stay away from men."

"They didn't stay away from Shoe and Truett, did they?" Willis asked.

"They wasn't camped, like we are," Cole said. "A wolf won't come near a fire."

"It better not," Willis said, putting his hand on his rifle. "I'll blow its head off."

Cole handed Willis a cup of coffee.

"Drink that before you freeze to death."

"We shoulda brought some beans," Willis complained.

"The beans was with the horse we didn't find," Cole said. "Just drink the coffee and keep your eyes open. I'm gonna get some sleep."

Clint handed Evie a plate of beans, then got some for himself.

"You're cold," she said.

"You bet."

"You should get some skins, like me and Jesse."

"How about after this I just stay out of Montana?" he asked. "Arizona and California are a lot warmer."

"Should we bring some beans to Jesse?"

"No," Clint said, "he'll have some when I relieve him."

She ate the beans ravenously.

"Aren't you tired?" he asked.

"No," she said, "I'm wide awake. You wanna get some sleep, go ahead. I know you're a lot older than I am."

"Yeah, that's a fact," he said around a mouthful of beans. "I am that."

"How old are you, anyway?" she asked.

"Like you said," he answered, "I'm older than you, but younger than Jesse."

"Jesse," she said. "How old is he, do ya think?"

"Now that," Clint said, "is something I've been wondering myself. I just can't tell."

THIRTY-FIVE

They decided to let Evie relieve Jesse so he could come to the fire, warm up, and have something to eat. Clint could have slept, but decided not to. He sat at the fire with Jesse and had coffee while Jesse finished the beans.

"You didn't really shoot the pups, did you?" Clint asked.

Jesse hesitated, then said, "No. But don't tell Evie."

"You couldn't do it, huh?"

"I aimed but I fired above them. They jumped, but didn't scatter. There's three of them, like I said. I thought leavin' them alive might bring the mother and father back."

"You're probably right," Clint said, "but you still couldn't do it."

"Shut up."

"The big white hunter."

"I'm warnin' you."

Clint let it drop.

"What about our friends out there?" Clint said. "Are you still willing to let them make the first move?"

"Sure, why not?"

"I could find them, sneak into their camp—"

"No."

"Why not?"

"Because while you're sneakin' around in the woods, one of the wolves could get you," Jesse said. "I'm more concerned with the animals than with the men."

"Okay," Clint said. "It's your hunt."

"Then get some sleep," Jesse said. "I'll be awake a while."

"Okay," Clint said, "when you get sleepy let me know. I'll keep watch."

"Sure thing."

Watching the mouth of the cave, Evie saw that Jesse was right. There was plenty of light by the moon for her to see. It was cold, but she was comfortable in her skins. Only her hands, holding her rifle, were cold.

She was glad she had confessed to Clint and Jesse that she'd never killed a wolf. It was better to be with them without the lie hanging over her head.

She thought she heard something, jerked her head around, and listened. If something was moving around out there, it was doing it quietly. She didn't hear another sound.

But then she thought she saw a shadow.

Cole sat and watched while Willis went to sleep. He wasn't keeping watch for men as much as he was for a wolf. He wasn't as confident as he had let Willis believe about the wolves not coming into camp, not after the way Shoemaker and Truett had been killed. He drank his coffee with one hand, held his pistol in his other, and kept his rifle across his knee.

He felt he was ready for anything.

Evie stood up, holding her rifle at the ready. She listened, squinted her eyes, looked toward the mouth of the cave—and saw them.

Both of them.

The white wolf was the largest, therefore she assumed it was the male. He remained outside the cave as the female went in. Apparently he was keeping watch while she checked on the pups.

Evie could have taken a shot, but she was enthralled by the magnificence of the white beast. Also, she couldn't help but feel sorry for the mother, who had gone inside and would soon discover the dead bodies of her pups.

She wondered if she would react the way a human mother would—with screams.

THIRTY-SIX

"He didn't do it!"

Clint looked at Evie. He had just come to relieve her and send her back to camp.

"What are you talking about?"

"They came back," she said.

"The wolves?"

She nodded.

"Both of them?"

"Yes," Evie said. "They went inside. And they didn't come running out. There was no sound. Surely if the pups were dead we'd know it. The mother would have come runnin' out, wouldn't she?"

"Yeah, okay," Clint said. "He didn't kill them. He figured if he left them alive the mother and father would come back."

"And they did," she said. "They're inside. Now. I . . . I could've taken a shot at the big white. I could see him clearly. But he was too . . . beautiful."

"I'll get Jesse," Clint said.

"But why?"

"Because this is his hunt," Clint said. "He has to decide what to do next."

She grabbed his arm as he started away. "Couldn't we let them go?" she asked. "The whole family of wolves?"

"But would they go?" Clint asked. "They've already killed a lot of stock, and two men. What about that, Evie?"

"I know."

"This is Jesse's job," Clint said. "He has to make the decision."

"All right. You go and get him," she said. "I'll stay and watch."

Clint started away, then stopped and looked back at her.

"No."

"No . . . what?" she asked.

"I'll stay," he said. "You go and fetch Jesse."

"Why? What do you think I'd do while you were gone?" she asked.

"Something stupid," he said. "Go."

Just then they heard it.

Howling.

Cole sat up straight as the howling came to him.

Willis also sat straight up, instantly awake.

"What the hell?" he said.

"A wolf."

Both men stood up, guns ready.

"Where is it?" Willis asked, looking around.

"Sounds pretty far off," Cole said.

"Says you," Willis retorted. "I'm not goin' back to sleep."

"Yeah, I'm not goin' to sleep, either."

Willis grabbed Cole's arm. "Come on, Cole," he said. "Let's either kill Trapp or get out of here."

Cole looked at Willis. Maybe he was right. Maybe he should have taken care of this long ago, even in Little Town, instead of waiting. Now there were wolves to deal with.

"Okay," he said. "Okay, Dave. We'll do it tomorrow."

Jesse heard the howling and came running. He joined Clint and Evie.

"You heard it," Clint said.

"I think people heard that a long way off."

"Why is it howling?" Evie asked. "You didn't kill the pups."

Jesse looked at Clint.

"I didn't tell her," he said. "She figured it out. The two wolves are in the cave."

"Now?"

Evie nodded.

"They came back. I . . . I couldn't take a shot."

"That's not your job," Jesse said, hefting his Sharps. "It's mine."

"So if the pups aren't dead, why did it howl?" Evie asked.

"Whether it's the male or the female," Jesse said, "it can tell that a human was in the den. They can smell me."

"So what will they do?"

"They'll take the pups, abandon the den, and find another one." Jesse got down on one knee, held his Sharps ready. "And when they come out, I'll be here."

THIRTY-SEVEN

Clint and Evie waited with Jesse.

The sun came up.

The wolves did not appear.

"You said there was no other way in or out," Clint said.

"That I saw," Jesse said.

"So you're sayin' there might be another way out?" Evie said.

"They could have found a way, a tunnel they could fit through."

"We'll have to find out for sure," Clint said. "I'll go in. If they're in there, I'll flush them out. If not, we'll have to keep hunting."

"What if they just leave?" Evie asked. "Will you pursue them if they leave the area?"

"I've been hired to hunt and kill the white wolf," Jesse said. "I won't stop until I've done that—and, if he has a pack with him, them, too."

"But that's not fair! What did the pups do? And the mother?"

"The mother may have done some killin', as well as her mate," Jesse said.

"No!" Evie said. "It's not fair."

She turned and ran for the mouth of the cave.

"Evie!" Clint shouted.

Cole and Willis mounted up and rode toward Trapp's camp. Cole fully intended to kill the man, but when they reached the camp no one was there.

"What the—" Willis said.

"They must be after the wolves," Cole said. "Let's leave our horses here and go on foot."

They rode the horses away from camp, then tied them off and went on foot. They were able to follow the tracks in the snow to the cave.

"There," Cole said. "They're waiting outside that cave."

They watched as Evie suddenly broke away and ran for the cave.

"Evie!" Clint Adams shouted, and went after her.

Jesse Trapp stayed where he was.

"Okay," Cole said. "Trapp is alone. Now we're gonna take him."

Clint tried to catch Evie before she ran into the cave, but she was too fast. He had no choice but to go in after her. He looked around for the torch Jesse had used. He saw it in the snow and picked it up, hoping there was still enough oil on it. He flicked a lucifer to life with his nail, held it to the end. For a moment he thought it wouldn't take, but suddenly it flamed on.

He held the torch high and went into the cave.

Cole and Willis moved around behind Jesse, intending to come up behind him. They moved as slowly as they could, but snow crunched beneath their feet. The hunter's keen hearing alerted him, and he turned.

"Who the hell are you?" he demanded.

"My name's Cole West," Cole said. "Does the name West mean anythin' to you?"

"No," Jesse said. "Should it? Are you the one who's been followin' me?"

"That's right," Cole said. "I've been followin' you." I'm gonna kill you."

"Why? I don't even know you."

"Your brother, John Henry," Cole said, "he killed both my brothers."

"If John Henry killed them," Jesse said, "they probably had it comin'."

"And he has it comin'," Cole said.

"Then go try to kill him."

"I can't find him," Cole said, "but when you walked into that saloon in Little Town and started tellin' your stories, I knew it was fate."

"Wasn't no such thing," Jesse Trapp said. "It was just a bunch of tall tales."

"Yeah, but your tales told me who you were."

"Then why didn't you try to kill me then?" Jesse asked. "Were you afraid?"

"It doesn't matter," Cole said. "I'm gonna kill you here and now."

"You and your friend," Jesse said, "go ahead and take your best shot."

THIRTY-EIGHT

As Evie entered the cave she immediately realized her mistake. It was dark, and she couldn't see. She tripped on a rock and fell to her knees. She scraped her palms as she put her hands out to catch herself.

"Damn!" she swore.

She hesitated, figuring her eyes might adjust to the darkness, but there was no hint of light in the cave. She was virtually blind.

Clint entered the cave with the torch held out in front of him. He heard Evie stumbling around ahead of him, then heard her swear. He knew she had to be blind.

"Evie, stay still," he said. "I'll come and get you."

"Clint?"

"I have a torch," he said. "Just stand still until I get there."

"Okay."

He moved forward, hoping he'd find her before one of the wolves did.

Evie was thinking about the pups, thinking of them as babies who needed her. Maybe she should just keep moving forward with her hands out ahead of her, and Clint would catch up.

She started to move, then stopped when she heard something ahead of her.

Growling.

She froze.

Clint kept moving until he saw Evie up ahead of him. She was standing still, like a statue. As he reached her the light from his torch spread out ahead of her, and illuminated a gray wolf baring its teeth. When struck by the light, though, the animal turned and ran farther into the cave.

"That was the mother," Evie said.

"You were ten seconds from having your throat torn out," he told her.

"God."

"Let's go back," he said. "The wolves are still in here. We have to go back and tell Jesse."

That was when they heard the shots. Clint turned and started running with Evie close behind.

The first shot from Jesse's Sharps struck Dave Willis in the stomach, and tore out his back in a spray of blood and guts.

Cole drew his gun, threw himself to one side, and

fired. The bullet seemed to be swallowed up by Jesse's skins, but didn't slow the man down. He leapt to the side, reaching inside his skins for his pistol while still holding on to his rifle.

Cole pulled the trigger five more times, hoping to catch Jesse at least one more time. Ducking down behind a rock, he quickly dumped the empty shells from his gun and quickly reloaded.

Jesse was able to reload his Sharps, sticking his pistol underneath his arm as he did so. Only then did he holster the pistol.

He and Cole both remained silent, listening. There was no sound from Willis as his blood stained the snow red.

Clint came running out of the cave, discarding the torch as he went. Evie came out behind him, holding her rifle ready.

"Stay here," he told her.

"But—"

"Stay here!"

"But . . . the wolves."

"They won't come out," he said. "Not while this commotion is going on."

She hoped he was right.

Cole saw Clint Adams come out of the cave and cursed to himself. He'd let Willis push him into this, and it had gone bad. Now he had to get away. He couldn't face Trapp and Adams, not alone.

He rose into a crouch and started firing as he ran.

* * *

Jesse stuck his head up to see what was happening. That was when Cole started to fire. He ducked back down. He became aware of a searing pain in his side, but put it out of his mind.

For the moment . . .

Clint was coming down the slope when Cole began to fire. He ducked, saw Cole running in a crouch. He also saw Jesse crouched down behind a boulder. He ran over and joined his friend. "What happened?" he asked.

"This feller showed up, said they wanted to kill me because John Henry killed his brothers."

"You know him?"

"No."

"What's his name?"

"West . . . um, Cole West, I think. You know that name?"

"No," Clint said, "never heard it."

"Where is he?" Jesse asked.

"Looks like he ran off," Clint said. "Want to try to track him?"

"No," Jesse said.

"We could probably do it easy in this snow—"

"I can't!"

"Why not?"

Jesse looked at Clint. "I think I got a bullet in me."

THIRTY-NINE

"Let me see."

Jesse pulled his skins aside. He had a bullet wound in his left side. "Hurts," he said.

"Doesn't look too bad," Clint said. "I'll have to see if the bullet is still in there."

Clint waved at Evie to come down. She did so, on the run.

"Is he all right?"

"He got hit by a lucky shot," Clint said. "We have to get him back to camp."

"Who shot him?"

"Later. Help me get him up."

"What about the wolv—"

"Later!" Clint snapped.

Together they managed to walk Jesse back to camp and set him down by the fire. As they walked past the dead man she looked down at the body, but did not ask any questions.

*   *   *

Cole made it back to the horses. He took what he thought he needed from Willis's horse, loaded it onto his own, then mounted up. He decided to go back to Wolf Creek and wait. Eventually Trapp and Adams would come back, after they had tracked and killed the wolf. After that they'd probably split up. That was when he'd take Jesse Trapp.

"I need some water," he said. "Melt some snow in the coffeepot."

"Okay."

"Roll onto your side," Clint told Jesse. The man obeyed. "No exit wound. You've got lead in there. I'll have to get it out."

"Okay."

He used the melted snow to clean the wound, then held the blade of Jesse's knife over the flames.

"Evie, you'll have to stay on watch."

"For the wolves?"

"For a man, or the wolves," Clint said.

"And if I see any?"

"Take the shot."

"Who's the man?"

"Just somebody looking for some revenge."

"Against Jesse?"

"Jesse's brother, but Jesse was handy."

"Can we—"

"No more questions, Evie. Keep watch while I get this bullet out."

"All right."

Clint leaned over Jesse. "You ready?"

"As I'll ever be. I've seen you do this before, years ago."

"Yes."

"You any better at it?"

"Probably not."

Jesse winced.

"Go ahead."

"Want something to bite down on?" Clint asked.

"Naw, that don't help," Jesse said. "Just do it!"

Clint felt with his fingers first for the bullet, located it, then probed with the tip of the knife.

"You're right," Jesse said, halfway through, "you ain't any better at this." He passed out.

"Is he—"

"He's just out," Clint said. "I've . . . almost . . . got it."

He got the bullet out, held it up to her so she could see it, then tossed it away. He used the rest of the water to clean the wound, then bandaged it tightly because he couldn't stitch it. Then he did his best to get Jesse comfortable and warm, keeping him by the fire and wrapping him in a blanket.

"Now what?" she asked.

"We keep him warm," Clint said, "don't move him for a while, and keep a sharp eye out."

"For man or beast?"

"Right."

FORTY

After dark, Jesse began to shiver and sweat.

"He's got a fever," Clint said. "He needs another blanket." He took the one he had wrapped around himself and added it to the one already covering Jesse.

"You want mine?" she asked from across the fire.

He looked at her all wrapped up and said, "No, you'll freeze."

"Well, you're gonna freeze," she said. "Come over here and we'll share."

He looked at her for a few moments, then said, "Okay, thanks."

He walked around the fire to her, poured two coffees first, then sat next to her. She spread her arms. He grabbed the edge of her blanket and pulled on it until it covered them both. He snuggled closer to her so that their bodies touched.

"Body heat's the best thing," he said.

"Right."

Clint thought he could feel the heat of her body even through her skins. Her face was dirty and her skins smelled, but she was a young, vibrant woman and snuggling up to her like that was making him aroused. There could have been a man in the dark getting ready to shoot at them, or a wolf getting ready to strike, and he was feeling randy.

And maybe she was, too.

She leaned over against him, put her head on his shoulder.

"I'm glad he didn't kill those pups," she said.

"We might still have to," he said.

"Not you," she said.

"Why not?"

Her hand fell into his lap, touched his thigh.

"You're too gentle," she said. "You wouldn't kill them."

She started to stroke his thigh; he could feel the heat from her hand.

"You sure of that?"

"Oh, yeah," she said. "I don't have a lot of experience, ya know, with men, but you . . . you're special."

"I am, huh?"

He wasn't sure she even knew what she was doing as she touched his thigh, but then her hand came into contact with his hard cock through his pants. She froze, and for a moment he thought she'd pull her hand away, but then she left it there. The warmth of her hand juts made him get harder . . . and then she began to rub him.

"Evie—"

She removed her hand, undid the front of her skin

and her shirt. Then she took his right hand in both of hers and pushed it inside her shirt. Her flesh was hot; the nipple of her small, firm breast was hard. When she let go of his hand, he left it there. She moved her hand back to his erection and squeezed him.

"It'll help us stay warm," she said.

He squeezed her breast, rubbed his palm over her nipple in a circular motion, then did the same to the other breast, and all the while they kept everything under the blanket, where the heat began to increase. She was right. The sexual excitement was making them warmer— hotter.

But if she kept squeezing him, and rubbing him, he was going to make a mess inside his pants.

"Evie," he said, putting his left hand over hers to stop her, "enough." He removed his hand from her naked breasts. "Button your shirt."

"But—"

"It's hot enough under this blanket," he told her.

He had put down his coffee cup to touch her breasts. Now he picked it up again.

"Clint—"

"You're very young."

"Old enough," she said. "I think you can tell that . . . can't you?"

"Okay, so you're a young woman, but this isn't the time or the place."

"Then when is?" she asked. "When we get back to Wolf Creek?"

"Maybe" he said. "Why don't you get some sleep? I'll keep watch."

She leaned over and put her head on his shoulder.

"It's nice and warm in here. I'll sleep right here," she said, and in moments, she was.

Clint didn't mind. He was warm, and he had access to the coffee, and his gun. And he was able to keep an eye on Jesse.

He wondered if the wolves would stay in the cave, or use the night to creep off and find another home?

FORTY-ONE

Oddly, Jesse woke before Evie did the next morning.

"Ow!" he said as he tried to move. "What happened?"

"You got shot. Remember?"

Jesse frowned, then said, "Yeah. How bad?"

"Could have been worse," Clint said. "You took a bullet in your side. I dug it out. I don't think it hit anything vital. In fact, I may have done more damage with your knife than the bullet did."

"Yeah, I figured," Jesse said. He flinched, then sat up. "She sleep like that all night?"

"Yeah," Clint said. "Pretty much. I'm warm, but my left arm is asleep."

"Well, wake her up and tell 'er to make breakfast," Jesse said. "Then we can get a move on."

"I'll wake her and she'll make breakfast," Clint said. "but you're not going anywhere for at least another day."

"Those wolves ain't gonna wait."

"They may be gone."

"Well," Jesse said, "if I can't move, that's gonna be up to you to find out."

While Evie made them some breakfast and looked after Jesse, Clint climbed back up the slope to the cave. He once again retrieved the fallen torch and was able to relight it. He entered the cave and, by the light, was able to determine that the wolves were gone.

He went back to camp with the news.

"The pups, too?" Evie asked, passing him a cup of coffee.

"Yes," Clint said. "All of them."

She looked at Jesse, who was already working on some beans and bacon. "So it didn't matter if there was another way out of that cave or not," she said. "They must have left in the dark."

"Now we'll have to track 'em," Jesse said.

She handed Clint a plate of hot food. "Why not just let them go?"

"Who says they're goin'?" he asked. "Maybe they're lookin' for somebody—or somethin'—else to kill."

She sat back with a plate of her own. "Okay, so what if we track them and they're movin' away from Wolf Creek?"

"Then they're somebody else's problem, is that what you're sayin'?" Jesse asked.

"Yes."

"Well, you're wrong," he said. "I can't just let them go to some other town and start killin' again. So, if they're movin' away from Wolf Creek you can stay home, but Clint and I will be goin' after them."

"And what about the man who shot you?" she asked.

"We'll be going after him, too," Clint said. "I'm not going to wait for him to strike first this time."

"No, I guess you're right about that," Jesse said. "We can't take a chance on him getting more help. We'll have to take care of him quick."

"So you'll track him, too?" she asked.

"Yes," Clint said.

"Then I'll come along."

"He'll probably head back to town," Jesse said.

"So we should head back, too," Evie said.

"First," Jesse said, "we'll have to find the wolf tracks and see which way they're goin'."

"I can do that," she said, "while you recover."

"I think Clint should do it."

"Why? Don't you trust me?"

Jesse grinned at her.

"I trust you to find those pup's tracks and cover 'em up to try and save 'em, Evie."

She frowned, but didn't try to deny it.

"Clint," Jesse said, "you got me wrapped up pretty tight. Maybe I can—"

"Not a chance," Clint said. "You're going to stay still until tomorrow. I'll go out today and look for some tracks."

"You'll go out now," Jesse said.

Clint looked down at his empty plate and his empty cup. "Okay," he said, "I'll go now."

"And I'll have more breakfast," Jesse said, holding

his plate out to Evie. "If I'm gonna stay here and recover, I'll need to eat more."

She took the plate, filled it, and handed it back.

Clint picked up his rifle and went off to find some tracks.

FORTY-TWO

When he returned a couple of hours later he was happy to see that Jesse was asleep, and Evie was alert. She was holding her rifle ready as he entered the camp.

"You can lower the rifle now," he said.

"I just . . . heard something . . . didn't know it was you."

"Well, you do, now." He got himself some coffee, hunkered down by the fire. "How is he?"

"He's been asleep since you left," she said. "What did you find?"

He drank down some hot coffee, then said, "We won't have to worry about that fellow Cole West coming back."

"Why not?"

He told her . . .

When Clint had left camp he quickly located the tracks left by the family of wolves. As he followed them, though, they suddenly intersected with tracks being left by a man on a horse.

The wolves continued to trail the horse when suddenly the tracks mixed, and Clint saw drops of blood in the snow. From there he followed the tracks and the blood. He assumed someone had been injured—either the wolves had injured the man or the man had injured one of the wolves—and then they continued on.

He kept his gun ready and remained alert in case a wolf came at him from another direction, but eventually he found something,

A horse.

The animal was breathing nervously while blood leaked from the saddle. The animal didn't look injured, but the smell of blood kept it skittish. Clint approached, spoke to it, and eventually was able to pat its neck and calm it down. He went through the saddlebags and found a letter addressed to Cole West.

If the animal was here that meant that its owner, West, was on foot. And if he was on foot he was as good as dead. Clint removed the saddle and tossed it away, so the horse would not continue to smell blood. If he let the horse loose it might run into the wolves, or it might make its way back to Wolf Creek. He decided to cut the animal loose. After all, it was a mustang.

Once the horse ran off Clint continued to track the man. He was on foot, leaking blood, and being followed by the wolves.

Eventually he came to a section of snow that was soaked with blood, then what looked like a trail left by a man dragging himself. Ultimately, he found the man, lying in the center of a pool of bloody snow. His throat had been torn out, and there were several other wounds. It looked as if the whole pack—father, mother, and pups—now had a taste for blood . . .

"Did you bury him?"

"No," Clint said, "I didn't want to take the time."

"Why?"

"I think we should get moving."

"But you said Jesse should rest."

"I know, but we've got a family of wolves that have tasted blood. I don't think they're going to go away. Not while we're here."

"Yeah, but three of them are pups."

"Evie, what you call pups are probably just smaller wolves. The father or mother will probably take the prey down, but then those pups will be on it. On us, if we wait around for them."

"B-but, that's . . ."

"I'm going to wake Jesse and see if we can get him on his horse," Clint said. "You get yours and his saddled. Douse the fire, first."

Clint went to Jesse while Evie poured the remnants of the coffee on the fire, then kicked snow on it.

"Wha—" Jesse said, coming awake.

"How you feeling, Jesse?" Clint asked.

"Stiff," he said. "I think yer probably right about waitin' another day—"

"Yeah, I was, but I changed my mind."

He told Jesse about finding Cole West dead, just about devoured by the entire family of wolves.

"Those wolves are hungry," Jesse said, "and those pups were a decent size—like a big dog. Yer probably right about movin' now. Just help me get on my horse."

They got the horses saddled, and then Clint boosted Jesse up onto his gray. He handed Jesse his Sharps.

"How do you feel?" he asked.

"I don't think I'm gonna fall off," Jesse said.

"You won't fall off," Clint said confidently.

He mounted up, rode up alongside Evie. "Let's keep him between us," he said to her in a low voice, "just in case he starts to fall off."

FORTY-THREE

Clint knew they wouldn't get back to Wolf Creek that day. They had broken camp and left too late. But maybe they could put some distance between themselves and the wolves.

But they soon knew that wasn't going to happen.

When they heard the howl, they stopped.

"They're followin' us," Jesse said.

"How do you know?" Evie asked.

"I can feel it," he said, "and that sound is right behind us."

"They followed West until they got him," Clint said. "There was blood all over his saddle. The wolf took him right off the horse's back."

"They're gonna come for us, Clint," Jesse said.

"They?" Evie asked.

Jesse nodded.

"Yeah, the whole family of wolves."

"The pups?"

"You didn't see the pups, Evie," Jesse said. "They're already the size of big dogs."

"I thought—"

"Yeah," Jesse said, "you thought they were babies."

She swallowed nervously.

"So we have five wolves tracking us?"

"They probably already have us surrounded," Jesse said.

"So what do we do?" she asked.

"We find a clearin' somewhere and make a stand," Jesse said.

"Okay," Clint said. "Let's hope we find one before they strike."

They did. They found it just up ahead, only it already had bodies in it.

"My God!" Evie said.

"These men must have been with West," Clint said. "There was four of them. You got one, Jesse, and the wolves got the other three."

"This is already a killing ground," Jesse said. "Let's do it here."

"We have to stay here?" Evie asked. "With all this blood?"

"It'll attract them," Jesse said, "excite them even more."

There was another howl.

"That's the female," Jesse said. "They're getting ready. We better dismount."

"Aren't we easy prey on foot?" she asked.

"We're not gonna be easy prey, Evie," Jesse said.

"We're gonna be waitin' for them, but we gotta let the horses and the mules go so they can defend themselves, if need be."

Clint and Evie dismounted, then helped Jesse out of his saddle.

"I better get on my knees," Jesse said. "So I don't keel over."

Clint slapped the horses on the rump, the mule a little harder to get it going. It wouldn't go far, not with the supplies on its back. Eclipse would not go far, either. Clint knew he should have unsaddled them and unpacked the mule, but he didn't think they had time. Jesse said the wolves were tightening the circle.

"They think we're easy prey," he said. "They think they've herded us here."

"Let's all get on our knees, back to back," Clint said. "Guns ready."

Jesse opened his skins so he could get to his pistol. Evie held her rifle ready. Clint had his rifle close, but when they came he would use his Colt. He'd use the rifle to finish them.

"Will they come before dark?" Evie asked

"I hope so," Jesse said. "If not, we'll have to build a fire."

"Won't that keep them away?" Evie asked.

"Not these wolves," he said. "Not the white one."

They heard movement in the trees and bushes around them.

"They're circlin'," Jesse said, cocking the hammer on his Sharps. "They're comin'. I want one shot at that white."

"Clint . . ." Evie said.

"Don't let the size of the wolf affect you, Evie," he said. "It'll tear your throat out if it gets a chance. Just shoot when they come in."

"Okay, I will," she said nervously.

"You'll be fine, Evie," he assured her.

It started to get dark and they were beginning to think they might have to build a fire.

And then they came.

There was a howl, very long, and Jesse said, "That's the male. They're comin'. Get ready!"

Clint kept his eyes open, his hand on his gun. He had to concentrate on what was happening in front of him, not behind him. Jesse and Evie were on their own.

A big gray wolf appeared from the brush and came straight for him. Her eyes glittered, muzzle wet with saliva dripping down. Behind her came two smaller wolves.

They came *fast*!

He drew his gun.

Evie also saw a gray wolf break from the brush and come at her. She saw what Jesse meant. This one was the size of a big dog. But it had evil eyes, unlike any dog she'd ever seen.

And its muzzle was still red with blood.

She raised her rifle.

The white came for Jesse.

It had blood on its muzzle, and in patches on its

white coat. Jesse thought one of those patches was an actual wound.

He raised his Sharps.

Clint drew and hired. A bullet hit the female, but she kept coming. He fired again. She screamed and went down. Behind her the two pups howled, but when Clint's shots hit them they screamed instead, and went down.

Evie hesitated, and it almost cost her. The wolf leapt and was in the air when she fired. Her bullet hit it in the chest. Its leap carried it into her, but when it collided with her, it was already dead.

The white wolf was a magnificent beast, Jesse thought, as he pulled the trigger of his Sharps. A .50-caliber hunk of lead had struck the wolf in his white chest. It was as if the animal's chest exploded, and the impact of the slug flung it back. It landed hard, adding blood to the already red snow.

"Everybody okay?" Clint asked.

Evie flung the carcass of the dead wolf away from her and said, "Yes."

"Okay," Jesse said. "I got the white."

"I got a pup," Evie said.

"The mother and two pups," Clint said.

He stood up and walked to the fallen white to check it.

"Dead," he said.

"Hell yes, it's dead," Jesse said, reloading his Sharps.

They all stood and looked around. Eclipse was right at the edge of the clearing, waiting for Clint.

"I'll get the horses and the mule," he said. "Time to go back."

Watch for

THE DEAD RINGER

357th novel in the exciting GUNSMITH series
from Jove

Coming in September!

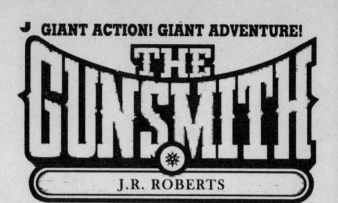

GIANT ACTION! GIANT ADVENTURE!

THE GUNSMITH

J.R. ROBERTS

Little Sureshot And
The Wild West Show
(Gunsmith Giant #9)

Dead Weight
(Gunsmith Giant #10)

Red Mountain
(Gunsmith Giant #11)

The Knights of Misery
(Gunsmith Giant #12)

The Marshal from Paris
(Gunsmith Giant #13)

Lincoln's Revenge
(Gunsmith Giant #14)

Andersonville Vengeance
(Gunsmith Giant #15)

penguin.com/actionwesterns

M455AS0510